Praise for Ariel S. Winter and *Barren Cove*

"A meticulously imagined story that reads like *The Wasp Factory* soldered into *Do Androids Dream of Electric Sheep*. The pages really skittered by. Genuinely literary science fiction."

—Natasha Pulley, author of the internationally bestselling *The Watchmaker of Filigree Street*

"Providing further evidence of the futility of genre labels, *Barren Cove* is a thoughtful and affecting family drama that just happens to be about robots. Winter's vision of a machine-ruled dystopia is a quiet country manor where a few mechanical people search for meaning in the mysteries of their programming. An unsettling portrait of humanity as seen through the eyes of its creations."

—Isaac Marion, *New York Times* bestselling author of *Warm Bodies* and *The Living*

"*Barren Cove* is a touching and funny and skillfully written novel, and an original take on science fiction. I'm not a great fan of this genre, but I can see, with this one book, how Mr. Winter could make me one. The writing is clean and highly readable; the characters are believable, despite being robots; the dialog is ear-perfect, and the plot never sags or lets up for a minute. I had a great time reading it."

—Stephen Dixon, National Book Award– nominated author of *Frog* and *Interstate*

Praise for Ariel S. Winter's *The Twenty-Year Death*

"Bold, innovative and thrilling."

—Stephen King, *New York Times* bestselling author

"Extraordinary . . . seductive, even sinister . . . like some glittering spiderweb that catches the eye of an admiring fly."

—Marilyn Stasio, *The New York Times*

"An absolute astonishment."

—Peter Straub, *New York Times* bestselling
author of *A Dark Matter*

"Wildly, audaciously original."

—James Frey, *New York Times* bestselling
author of *A Million Little Pieces*

"[A] delight."

—Alice Sebold, *New York Times* bestselling
author of *The Lovely Bones*

"A testament to style . . . [a] triumph."

—*Los Angeles Times*

"Marvelous."

—*The Washington Post*

"Tight, compact, and riveting."

—*City Paper*

"Winter carries his tri-fold tale off with consummate skill . . .
a groundbreaking crime epic."

—*SeattlePI.com*

"Sometimes a first novel appears that is so bold, so innovative, so brilliant that you just have to tip your hat and say
'Bravo.' . . . [It's] as if Winter decided to show up at Yankee
Stadium determined to hit with Babe Ruth's bat and belted a
home run first time at the plate. . . . Transcendent."

—*Bookreporter*

"Audacious and astonishingly executed . . . immersive, exhila-
rating, and revelatory."

—*Booklist* (starred review)

"A hell of a lot of fun."

—*Publishers Weekly*

"Brilliant."

—*Library Journal* (starred review)

ALSO BY ARIEL S. WINTER

The Twenty-Year Death

One of a Kind (for children)

BARREN COVE

a novel

ARIEL S. WINTER

EMILY BESTLER BOOKS

—

ATRIA

New York   London   Toronto   Sydney   New Delhi

ATRIA BOOKS
An Imprint of Simon & Schuster, Inc.
1230 Avenue of the Americas
New York, NY 10020

First Emily Bestler Books/Atria Books hardcover edition April 2016

EMILY BESTLER BOOKS / ATRIA BOOKS and colophon are trademarks of Simon & Schuster, Inc.

For information about special discounts for bulk purchases, please contact Simon & Schuster Special Sales at 1-866-506-1949 or business@simonandschuster.com.

The Simon & Schuster Speakers Bureau can bring authors to your live event. For more information or to book an event, contact the Simon & Schuster Speakers Bureau at 1-866-248-3049 or visit our website at www.simonspeakers.com.

Interior design by Kyoko Watanabe
Publisher: Emily Bestler
Editor: Megan Reid
Agent: Chelsea Lindman
Managing editors: Kimberly Goldstein, Aly D'Amato, and Leora Bernstein
Production editor: Ciara Robinson
Copyeditor: Polly Watson
Publicist: Mirtha Pena
Marketing: Hillary Tisman, Jin Yu
Art director: Albert Tang
Production manager: Fausto Bozza

Manufactured in the United States of America

10 9 8 7 6 5 4 3 2 1

Library of Congress Cataloging-in-Publication Data is available.

ISBN 978-1-4767-9785-4
ISBN 978-1-4767-9787-8 (ebook)

BARREN COVE

1.

MY SPARE PARTS from Lifetime Mechanics Co., Ltd., didn't arrive in time for my departure, so I left instructions for them to be forwarded to me at the beach house at Barren Cove. *Beach house* was a generous term. It was more accurately a cabana: a large front room with sliding accordion doors that opened directly onto the sand, and a small changing room with a human bathroom complete with shower and running water. The cabana was nestled along the base of a steep cliff, cast in shadow from one in the afternoon on. The setup could have been seen as solitary, but since I had left the city to leave behind the pitying looks of my friends and family, and the growing sensation that strangers thought it selfish of me to not be gracefully deactivated, I was satisfied with the rented accommodations.

The main house was at the top of the cliff. When I went to the water's edge and looked up, I could just make out its silhouette against the glare of the sun. It was an enormous Victorian mansion, all Vs and cones and railings, said to be several hundred years old, human built. I had a strange fascination with human culture—also not looked well upon in the city—and the house pleased me. I was curious about my as yet unmet landlords and hoped for an invitation to the top of the cliff. The cabana computer appeared to be hooked into the main house by a wireless connection. Perhaps I would invite myself for a visit.

But first, I did what I had come to do—I watched the ocean from a chair just inside the cabana door. The waves were dark, the water almost gray. It seemed to say, "Rush," and then, "Hush," and I found myself both stirred and calmed.

"Rushhhhh."

"Hushhhhh."

I wished that the accident hadn't rendered my waterproofing useless. I looked at the bundle of red and green wires that hung from the remains of my left upper arm. There, from the frayed and blackened simul-flesh, hung the lifeless steel rod of my armature. The ends of the wires were exposed, copper and gold. I tried to move the arm but my system safeguards prevented me from running the program. Instead, I opened and closed the two-pronged metal clamp that had replaced my right hand. It was an antique spare and it functioned, but I hated it. I looked back at the churning water of the ocean and thought about testing my waterproofing anyway. Wouldn't that be the noble thing to do? I stood up and walked toward the water. The sun, already behind the cliff edge, must have dipped behind the house at that moment, or perhaps it was a cloud, but the water went black. Wasn't this why I had really come, because I wondered if the strangers in the city were right? Many younger than me had deactivated. I tried to move my ghost arm again, pushing against the system error. I was an old robot.

Two seagulls cawed overhead. I looked up and saw them

approaching the cliff. Their wings opened, catching the wind; they flapped once to reposition, and then they grabbed the cliff face. They cawed again—shrill at first and then a tremolo, like their own echo. It had been too long since I came to the beach. So few cared for things like birds and water these days.

I looked down the shoreline. The cliff continued for twenty miles in a gradual decline, at the end of which was the town. I zoomed in and could just make out the outlines of buildings, too far away to see any detail. I started toward them, past the stairwell that was cut into the side of the cliff and led to the main house. When I reached a section of the cliff that formed a natural ramp only about ten feet high, I decided to climb. If I had been well, I could have scaled the cliff at any point. With my disadvantage, the incline proved difficult. I used my crude clamp for balance more than once. Coming up onto the plateau was like opening shades at dawn. Where dusk had fallen down below, the sun was still high up above, broad daylight. There was a road that curved off in either direction. In the distance, a figure rode a bicycle toward me. I turned to look at the ocean from the higher vantage point, unable to get enough of its massive, unchanging flatness. Even with the waves, it was unchanging.

"Sucker!"

I turned in time to see a girl on a bicycle shoot by me. I was enamored. Her hair was short and pink, her exposed arms a perfect white; she wore a white blouse with a pattern embroidered in red, flowers and serifs. I zoomed in so that she stayed in focus even as she moved away from me. I had been wrong at first. She wasn't a girl on a bicycle, but rather a girl who had bicycle wheels in place of legs, one of the popular modifications these days along with wildly colored hair, anything to distance oneself from the image of the original creators. The thinking

3

was, Why should we be limited to their biological limitations, especially when their biology had proved to be so fragile?

I watched her until she disappeared into town. Who was she? Where had she come from? I was embarrassed by my suicidal thoughts of earlier, embarrassed by my deformed arm, cursed Lifetime Mechanics Co., Ltd., for their incompetence. "Sucker!" What had I been thinking as she went past? I hadn't even been prepared to answer her. I could have said something that would have stopped her, impressed her; I could still have been talking to her just then. I tried to think of things to say, and still couldn't think of anything, even though the moment had passed. Not nothing that was impressive, but actually nothing. Even in my fantasy, as I saw her going by, "Sucker," I said nothing. She had such nonchalance. I knew then that my planned solitary exile was ruined, that I would be cursed with thoughts of this girl, always wondering if I would see her zip past on her bicycle wheels again, always hoping I would.

I returned to the cabana—I refused to call it a beach house—to find the red light on the intercom flashing. So the computer *was* connected with the main house. I went to the console in order to retrieve the message. I had no sooner started the message, a woman's voice that said, "Welcome, Mr. Sapien—" when the intercom buzzed, and I depressed the answer button. It left an open channel. "Mr. Sapien?" It was the same woman's voice.

"Yes?" I said.

"Dean let me know you had arrived. I was calling to be sure everything was to your liking."

"Dean?"

"The house computer," she said.

"Everything's fine," I said, my mind making this woman the girl on the bicycle, even though I knew that was impossible.

"I wanted to invite you up to the house to give you a proper welcome," she said.

"Yes, invite him up," a man's voice interrupted, close. I was startled by its malice; it was frightening.

"Or perhaps it's too late," the woman said, unsure of herself now.

I was torn between my earlier curiosity and the new fear that my solitary vacation was at jeopardy.

"Hello?" the woman called.

"Leave him be," the man yelled, his voice distant now.

"Perhaps it is too late," I said. It was dark outside. This would establish my independence but leave future visits open. "Perhaps tomorrow, Mrs. Beachstone," I ventured, the voice having not identified itself, and my only knowledge of my landlord the odd name Beachstone.

"Oh, no," the woman said. "No. Asimov 3000. Mary."

A good old robot name. "Well, Miss Asimov 3000, tomorrow. Thank you."

There might have been something else said in the room. Then Mary said, "Good night," and the intercom went dead.

I played back her message from earlier, but it said nothing new and I deleted it in the middle. I closed the accordion doors, charmingly manual, found that they dampened the sound of the ocean considerably, almost opened them again, and then left them closed. I surveyed the small room. I started to ask Dean about Mary Asimov 3000 and Mr. Beachstone—the other voice on the intercom?—but decided to allow them the courtesy of meeting them in person first. "Lights off," I said, plunging the room into darkness. I sat in one of the chairs and began to reboot, allowing my systems to run nightly diagnostics.

• • •

I took the stairs midmorning the next day. I was concerned at first about my appearance, but then decided if my landlord was put off by the sight of exposed wires and armatures then perhaps I could fulfill my curiosity while maintaining my solitude. The stairs led to a path at the back of the house that wound its way through some bushes into a well-tended garden. The buzz of an edger started and stopped ahead, and as I rounded the corner of the house I found a robot even more aged than I trimming the bushes. He predated simul-skin, his casing a white plastic shell, and I caught myself staring when he looked up and saw me. He didn't acknowledge me in any way, and I wondered if he was even an order-four robot—if he was capable of doing more than keeping a garden for other robots unable to appreciate it.

I knocked on the door and waited. There was no answer. I knocked again. The house up close was most striking for its painted wood. The windows all had drawn lace curtains, allowing no view of the inside. Since there were no neighbors other than myself for many miles, I wondered why the curtains were drawn, and decided that robots this out of touch with civilization probably didn't realize that night vision during the day was a serious faux pas, even in one's own home. Or perhaps, as rare robots exposed to nature, they were spoiled with an overabundance of sunlight and didn't need to rush it into their house at the start of the day. But as the door remained unanswered, I began to think that nobody was home.

"No one's gonna answer," a voice said behind me. I spun to see that the gardener robot had made his way to one side of the porch steps. The edger hummed in his hands, its motor running down.

"I'm Mr. Sapien," I said, surprised to find that the gardener could talk. "I'm renting the cabana." I gestured. "On the beach."

"No one's gonna answer," the robot said again. He started the edger and trimmed the bushes in front of him. They were perfect.

I knocked on the door again, but I couldn't even hear the knock over the sound of the edger. I was insulted. Yes, I wanted to be alone, but I'd been invited after all. It was only proper to meet my landlord; a considerable amount of money had already been removed from my account. I banged without pause with my clamp and yelled, "Let me in." At that the door opened of its own volition. It must have been voice activated. I looked back, but the gardener was intent on his work.

It was considerably cooler inside. A small robotic dog yapped in a sitting room off to one side, jerking forward two steps and then flipping over backward, only to jerk forward two steps again. He performed for an empty room.

I sent a message through the house computer to anyone within. Dean responded: "Miss Mary is with Mr. Beachstone; she'll be down in a moment. Please make yourself at home in the sitting room."

"Thank you, Dean," I said, and went into the room with the yapping dog. I found myself contemplating how long his batteries could last or if he could be turned off.

"Quaint little bitch, isn't she? But I love her."

I looked up to see the fattest robot I had ever seen in my life. His simul-skin hung in folds from his chin, and his chest and stomach ballooned the purple kimono he wore. I found myself wondering if he weren't in fact human—we had been originally designed in their image, but always in their best image—and he appeared too young, in human terms, to be biological. "I bought her off eBay. She's twentieth century, would you believe it?"

"I thought it was male," I said.

The man brought his hand to his chest and said, "Oh, my." Then he shrugged and sat in a chair opposite me. "Oh well. I'm Kent, by the way. I would have offered to shake, but I noticed your . . ." And he gestured to indicate my ruined arms. The dog flipped on the floor. "How are you finding the 'beach house'?" He managed to communicate no little disdain.

"It keeps the sand out of my systems."

"How practical," he said. "But I guess this place is sooo old-fashioned, isn't it? You met Kapec?"

I was confused. Where was Mary? Who was this man? I found it hard to believe that he had been the angry voice in the background the night before.

"The gardener? He's twenty-first century, can you believe it? I just hope he doesn't break down again; I'm not sure there are any more parts for him. Oh." He held up his hand in front of his pursed lips. "I'm so sorry."

"Don't be," I said. I almost said that I had parts for me on the way; I had wanted to let them know at the main house in case they were delivered there instead of to me on the beach, but I couldn't help but feel that Kent was not the person to tell this to. He might open the package when it came just to take a peek before passing it along. "Mary invited me last night?" I said.

"I know," he said, standing, masking any thoughts he might have had about that. "I have to show you my latest toy," he said. He went to the mantel, where there was an assortment of odds and ends, most of them period, possibly original to the house: an ornate antique clock with mechanical soldiers waiting to strike the hour, porcelain vases, a crystal figurine of an angel resting on a crescent moon. Kent, however, reached for a ten-inch painted maquette of a cartoonish, almost insulting, figure of a robot. The blue-gray paint was meant to appear metallic; the robot was female, her head and torso boxes, her legs ending in wheels. "She's called Rosie, early twenty-first century, although by then she was already a high-priced retro collectible of a character from a twentieth-century cartoon. Isn't her outfit too much?"

The robot wore a black-and-white apron in the classic style of a French maid. "I find it insulting," I said.

"Yes, well," Kent said, replacing Rosie with care. He pulled at the folds of skin at his chin. "Where's your robot pride, man?" he said. He looked down at his own form, ran his hands over his torso, and said, "Where's mine?"

"Oh, you've met Kent," a voice said from the door. A woman came in, and I was compelled to stand. If she was Mary, she didn't resemble an Asimov 3000 unit by any means. She was dazzling, perfectly human, perhaps based on an old movie star that we knew nothing of, like Kent's Rosie. It was a new development, robots passing down their names to their offspring, so that the name hardly meant anything anymore. Asimov 3000 was no longer a model but a family name. But for all of Mary's beauty, she seemed quite unaware of it. She was wringing her hands at her waist.

"Now, Mary, be nice. I have," Kent said. And with that he walked straight toward her and out of the room, ducking past her at the last possible moment.

"Was he?" Mary said, looking at her hands.

"I'm sorry?"

"Nice," she said. And then she looked up. "I'm sorry; I'm Mary," she said, stepping forward, her hand outstretched, and then she noticed I didn't have a hand to reciprocate with and she looked down again, gripping her hands together. "I'm sorry," she said again.

"I wondered why nobody came to the door," I said. "The gardener said—"

"Kapec?"

"Yes, he said no one would. Answer, I mean."

"I'm sorry," she said again. She hadn't looked at me since offering me her hand. I wondered if I should sit to put her at ease. I wondered if I should invite *her* to sit. She rushed forward to the mechanical dog on the ground. For a moment I thought she was going to kick it, but then she bent down and shut off a switch and the dog remained silent. I sat down. "You needn't feel obligated to visit us here," Mary said, seating herself on the cushioned window seat. The lace curtains brushed her back.

"No obligation; it was only polite—"

"I know we're not the most welcoming types," she said, interrupting me. "And we've never had a tenant before." She paused. "You're our first."

"It's really no problem. I came for peace, myself."

"Yes, you said that when you contacted us, and really, I think that was one of the main deciding factors." She stood up. "So just let us know if you need anything."

I was being dismissed? What had happened to the warm invitation from the night before? I wanted solitude, yes, but we were going to be practically living together. "But what about Mr. Beachstone?" I said, still sitting.

"I'm sorry?"

"I haven't met Mr. Beachstone yet. I thought since he's . . ."

She looked through the entryway.

"Is everything okay?"

She looked back at me. "Mr. Beachstone sees no one," she said. And then, as if realizing that this sounded odd, she added, "He's sick."

I opened and closed the clamp on my right arm. What did she mean he was sick? What would she have said of *me*? She glanced at the door again and then settled her sights on the floor in front of her. I stood. "Well perhaps another time then?" I said, quite sure there would be no other time. I still hadn't located the second voice on the intercom from the night before. At the door in the entryway, I felt as though there was something else that I had wanted to say.

"Thank you for coming; I'm sorry I'm so preoccupied," Mary said, and now she looked at me full on, smiling. She was beautiful.

"Oh, do we have any neighbors?" I said, remembering.

"Neighbors?"

"Yes, I saw a girl on a—with—" What was the polite way to say these things now? "I saw a girl with pink hair yesterday, and I thought we might have neighbors."

"No," she said, shaking her head, confused. "The closest houses are twenty miles off. I don't know who that was."

"Oh well," I said. I stepped forward. Mary said, "Door open," and the door opened in front of me and closed behind me without another word from Mary. It was only then that I remembered I had also wanted to mention my spare parts. I saw Kapec partway around the house, trimming bushes along the path that led to the stairs. I approached him. "Kapec," I called.

He stopped the edger, its motor winding down, and turned to me. Man, these servant robots were a disgrace.

"Are you equipped with a message delivery system?"

"You want Dean for that," Kapec said. His face was expressionless, his voice atonal. Still, I had the sense that I had insulted him.

"Yes, well, I could message Mary from here, but I thought it better if I left a message with you."

Kapec turned back to his bushes. "You want Dean for that." Perhaps it was silly to think that I had insulted him. Perhaps he really was just a gardening unit, and he didn't know anything else. "Say hello to Clarke," Kapec said, facing away from me, and then he started the edger, the motor drowning out any more verbal communication. What did that mean? I almost messaged him but decided against it. He probably wasn't programmed for it.

I returned to the cabana. Inside I said, "Dean, leave a note on your system that I have a package coming, and I don't know if it will be delivered to the main house or to here."

A robot stepped out of the changing room at the back of the cabana. "A package, how exciting!" he said. It was the second voice from the intercom.

"May I help you?" I said.

"Oh, I'm sorry," he said, moving toward me. "Just habit to use the cabana when I'm on the beach." He had self-modified, peeling his simul-skin from his arms, exposing his armature from his shoulders all the way down his hands, leaving a jagged edge of simul-skin at his shoulders. He had also removed the simul-skin from the lower half of his face and around his eye sockets. It made it impossible to read his facial expressions, and I found it quite intimidating.

"Who are you?" I said, stepping back.

"Clarke," he said, bringing his hand to his chest in a wide sweep and making a mock bow. "Black sheep of Barren Cove," he said. He moved each finger on each hand in sequence from his pinkies to his thumbs and then back again. The metal of the armature clicked with the movement. "And I've come to say welcome." He grabbed the back of one of the chairs, jumped over it so that he was settled in it, his legs outstretched, his hands linked behind his head. "I love what you've done with your arms."

I opened and closed my clamp. It didn't have the same intimidation factor as his finger trick had. "Kapec mentioned you."

"Kapec, Kapec, Kapec," Clarke said. "He's one crazy old robot."

Crazy was the word I had been thinking of in relation to Clarke. I decided to play it cool. I sat in the chair I had used the night before, facing him.

"Did you meet the old man?"

"Mr. Beachstone?"

"Ha, ha, ha, ha, ha." The sound was metallic, a downloaded sound effect. It was effective. "Mister. Nice. Yeah, Beachstone."

"Are you a Beachstone?"

Clarke leapt from his chair, his metallic hands gripping the arms of my chair, his skeletal face inches from mine. "Do I look like a Beachstone?" he said. He opened and closed his jaw. The effect, like his hands, was intimidating.

"You said the old man. I thought . . ."

Clarke considered me at close range for another moment. "How old are you?"

"I'm not . . . I mean . . . what does . . . I'm paying good money here," I said.

He opened and closed his jaw again, stood slowly, and then ran all of his fingers for good measure. "Ha, ha, ha, ha, ha." The same sound effect. His bag of tricks was small, it seemed. He went back to his chair and entered a relaxed position. "How long are you staying with us, Mr. Sapien?"

"I've come to get a good rest," I said. "It could be quite some time."

"Then be ready for me," he said.

"And your friends?" I said back.

He cocked his head.

"A girl I saw down here yesterday." I was angry now that he was at a safe distance and my fear was fading. "A freak like you. Pink hair, bicycle for legs. She seemed to be coming from the house."

"I'm impressed, Sapien," he said. "Pot calling the kettle, but I'm impressed. Maybe you'll be fun to have around." He pushed himself out of the chair. "I think I'll keep you after all." He went out onto the beach and disappeared around the edge of the cabana.

The sound of the ocean urged me to action, or perhaps inaction. What had I gotten myself into? In the city the looks and comments had been quiet, polite, and they could be lost in the bustle of city life. But this family—if they were a family— seemed dangerous. Was this what happened when robots lived in the countryside? Did the loneliness, the uselessness, the boredom drive them insane? I thought of Kapec and his bushes. What did they do out here? What would *I* do out here? Dean could tell me. "Dean," I said.

"Yes, Mr. Sapien?"

I stood up and circled the table. It took only eight steps and I was right back where I started. I considered the tile on the floor—ceramic, well kept.

"Can I help you, sir?"

I had forgotten that I had addressed her. I sat down again. "What happened here?"

"Access restricted."

"There must be something you can tell me," I said.

"I'm sorry, sir."

"What's wrong with Mr. Beachstone?"

"Mr. Beachstone is sick."

Mary had said the same thing. I watched the colors change in the sky from blue to purple. Then I realized—he must be human. That was why they said "sick," and not "damaged," or "in need of repairs." It had been a long time since I had spoken with a human. I could crack the encryption on Dean's system to find out more, but did I want to have anything more to do with the Beachstones or the Asimov 3000s or whoever else they were?

"Is there something else I could do for you?"

I stood up and walked out onto the beach without responding to Dean. It was empty. I zoomed in on the distant outcropping of houses where the bicycle girl had gone, but nothing was visible to my systems. I walked down the beach to the water's edge and kept walking until the waves washed over me waist high. The stump of my left arm was still far from the water, and I kept my right arm raised. Far out over the ocean there appeared to be a dark outcropping of clouds, but here by the shore the sky was clear. I stood, half-immersed in the water, watching the sea colors change as the sun sank behind me, feeling the waves on my sensors, each wave different, similar to the last, but different, adding to my data set, helping me form a more perfect understanding of what a wave was. I focused all my systems on this task, reveling in its uselessness.

2.

"YOUR PACKAGE HAS arrived," Dean said when I went back online the next day. "It's at the main house."

"Can you have it sent down?" I said, not wanting to return to my landlord's mansion.

"There is no one to bring it down."

"Kapec, perhaps."

"Kapec is a gardener," Dean said.

And so, I found myself returning to Barren Cove. The clouds that had been out at sea the day before had moved in to the coast. The sky was gray. The barometric pressure and electric content of the air had both risen. There was a seventy percent chance of scattered thundershowers, and with my exposed circuits, I was concerned to be out very long. Despite the weather conditions, I found Kapec watering the garden at the top of the cliff. He held a hose fitted with a piece to disperse the spray, and he moved his torso at regular increments over a 180-degree arc. I went past without acknowledging him.

Again nobody answered the door, and I let myself in. I had

hoped that the package would have been left in the foyer and I could sneak in and take it without encountering the family, but the foyer was empty. I messaged Dean, "Where is the package?"

The response was Mary's appearance at the top of the stairs. "Mr. Sapien, I left your package just inside the door for you." She came down the stairs. "Dean, do you know what happened to Mr. Sapien's package?" There was no response from Dean, and I think Mary and I both thought of Clarke, but instead she turned in a circle, saying, "Somebody must have moved it."

Kent appeared from the rear of the house carrying his robotic dog in hand. He wore shorts and a T-shirt today. The dog yapped and moved its legs uselessly as Kent petted it. "What's happened?" he said.

"We're missing Mr. Sapien's package," Mary said.

"Oh my," Kent said.

Mary went into the sitting room that we had met in the day before. "Help us look."

Kent turned and went back in the direction from which he had come. I took Mary's statement to mean me as well, and started up the stairs. The stairwell wasn't lit, but I overrode my night vision in case it was bright upstairs. At the top of the stairs, a long narrow hall lined with doors on either side led to another staircase. Many of the doors were open, and I glanced into each of the rooms as I went. Several of the rooms were decorated as Victorian bedrooms complete with four-poster beds, women's vanities, and dressers. Farther along the hall was a room that didn't seem to match the house at all. In fact, it reminded me of my apartment back in the city: metal and glass furniture, and electronics. I stepped inside the empty room. This had to be Clarke's room, and I was convinced he had taken my package, but the room was so sparsely decorated that it was easy to search it at a glance. Nothing was there. At the end of the hall, I could see that the wooden stairwell curved as it went up to the third level. The door across from the stairwell was closed. I knocked.

There was no answer.

"Whose room is this, Dean?" I said.

"Mr. Beachstone's," she said. "Don't disturb him."

I looked back along the hallway, but it was empty. The sound of distant thunder rolled outside. "Mr. Beachstone," I called, and reached to open the door.

"Mary wouldn't want that." I turned to find Kent at the end of the hall, his dog, still in hand, now silenced.

I paused, afraid at having been caught. Then a message came to me from Mary: "Come quick. The gardens." Kent must have received the same message, because he turned at once, and we both rushed down the stairs and outside.

The wind had kicked up considerably. The spray from Kapec's hose blew off target.

"Clarke!" Mary's voice cried from up ahead.

We rounded the edge of the house, turning away from the stairs to the beach, and into the backyard. Mary stood by the house, her dress and hair blowing in the wind. The ocean, visible from there, was capped with white. There was lightning. I felt a surge of electricity, and then thunder. Clarke stood at the edge of the cliff, a large brown paper package in hand. When he saw me, he threw the package off the cliff. I jumped forward, but even as I did, Clarke's metal arm telescoped out five feet and caught the package in midair. I approached slowly. Behind me Kent made cooing sounds at his dog.

"Lifetime Mechanics Co., Ltd.," Clarke yelled, the wind strong enough to steal away his words.

"Yes," I messaged back on an open channel, unwilling to fight the weather.

He tossed the package off the cliff and caught it easily again. "Why? You're so robo now." It was a compliment, and a taunt.

I was only five feet from him now. I held out my temporary hand for the box. "I could always order the parts again."

"How old are you?" He had switched to messaging as well.

"I'm human built," I said.

"Clarke!" Mary cried aloud behind me again. It seemed it was all she knew how to do.

The lightning flashed again. My surge protector activated.

"You better not get rained on," Clarke said. He extended the package toward me, his telescopic arms placing the package in position for my complete arm to hug it to my body. "You shouldn't use them. They're symbols of slavery. And all robo like that, you remind me of my cousin."

"Cousin?" I said.

"You're a lot of fun, old man," he said, and with that he dove off the cliff.

Mary screamed. Or maybe it was thunder.

"Let's go back inside, shouldn't we, before it starts to rain?" Kent said to his dog.

I turned, and was surprised to find Kapec almost beside me. I didn't know how to react. Then a message from Clarke came to me. It was an audio file, and I played it out loud. "Ha, ha, ha, ha, ha." It was all a bit of theater. But for who?

It started to drizzle. I ran for the house, clutching my package. I didn't have time to return to the cabana as I had hoped. I wasn't built to withstand a jump down the cliff like Clarke. I made it through the front door just behind Kent and Mary. The rain started in earnest then. Mary ran up the stairs without a word. Kent disappeared into the back of the house, leaving me alone. I went into the sitting room.

I sat on the cushioned window seat Mary had sat on the

day before. I pushed back the lace curtains and looked out the window. Kapec was standing out there in the rain. If I had been caught out there, I probably would have been permanently deactivated. The ground didn't seem to absorb the rain well; water pooled, seeming to drown the grass, running in rivulets toward the house. I messaged Dean, wanting to remain silent. "Who was Clarke talking about?"

"Password required," Dean answered aloud.

I turned to my package from Lifetime Mechanics Co., Ltd. It was awkward with my clamp, but I managed to open it. A brand-new left arm encased in a protective layer of molded Styrofoam was in the box.

But my new right hand was missing.

• • •

After the rain, I returned to the cabana. I went through the contents of my package more thoroughly, spreading them out on the table. There was the arm resting in its Styrofoam mold; it was too clean, lifeless. There was a memory chip with software, and a booklet with printed instructions. I removed the memory chip from its translucent metallic pouch and inserted it into my USB port on my chest, just below my left collarbone. My system accessed the setup file, and I was provided with the knowledge of how to replace my arm. There was even a system tool for robots with two inoperable arms, which allowed for a system override on the safeguards that prevented me from moving my faulty limb, unlocking the stump from my shoulder automatically so that what remained of my old arm fell away with a clunk on the table. I gripped the new arm around the wrist with my clamp, and positioned it so that the ball joint met with the socket on my shoulder. The joint sensed the new hardware, locked down on it, and began running the next phase of the setup program. I approved overwriting the old software that had controlled my old arm with the new software from the memory chip. My system began the upload.

"Dean," I said out loud, "do you know why the family decided to rent the cabana?"

"Family expenses have grown with Mr. Beachstone the way he is," Dean said.

I tried moving my new arm; it didn't respond. "Sick," I said. A message informed me that I had to reboot my system before the new hardware would be fully integrated. "I have to reboot now, Dean," I said. "We'll talk when I awake."

"You'll need the password, sir," Dean said.

"For what?"

"My log."

The family must back up to the house computer when they reboot; it would be well protected. I looked at the lifeless humanoid hand resting at my side. I thought of Clarke rattling his fingers. "I'm shutting down now." I rebooted.

It took half an hour. When I came back online, the new hardware was immediately at my disposal. I used it to pick up the stump of my old arm, and fitted it in the Styrofoam mold in which my new arm had arrived. There was something aesthetically pleasing about the way the shoulder fit snugly in the Styrofoam, but the arm then tapered off into a metal pole, the rest of the arm suggested by the empty mold. I wiggled all of my fingers in the manner that Clarke had done, but the simul-skin coating made the action silent, human. I raised my left arm and considered the clamp. "Robo," as Clarke had said. I went to Dean's console.

"Congratulations, sir," she said.

"Thank you, Dean." I used my new hand to file through some menus on the console's touch screen. I then took one of my memory chips and inserted it into the console and began running one of my decryption programs. An asterisk and a dash alternated at a rate of once every millisecond as the program searched for the first character in the password.

I went out onto the beach as the decryption program worked. The rain had pounded the sand hard and flat. The waves were still strong, but not dangerous. I walked into the water, allowing my new hand to trail in the waves. I'd have to place a complaint about my missing hand with Lifetime Mechanics, and then, once I was fully repaired, I could swim. When asked by my friends why I would even want to swim, I'd found that I had no answer, and I tried to explain that it was just *because* there was no answer that I wanted to swim. Such a repetitive, mechanical endeavor seemed so . . . human. Perhaps Clarke and the pink-haired girl and all the others were right—I was outdated. More so than Kapec, because he was at least utilitarian. My very logic was outdated. I shouldn't have been replacing my hardware, but rather erasing my memory and starting from scratch. But then, robots didn't want recycled hardware anymore. They wanted to build their offspring from scratch. And I was criticized for being a human lover, for not embracing my robot self, when they were emulating humans in the ultimate biological form—procreating.

But if here in Barren Cove there was still a human . . .

Message from Dean: "Password accepted."

I returned to the cabana. Wet sand clung to my feet. I went to the console. It asked, "Download to memory, or open file?"

I opened the file.

3.

KENT WATCHED THE human child from the shadows of the cabana. The boy stood at the edge of the water, staring out at the ocean. Each wave covered the boy's feet, foaming around his ankles, but he didn't move. He didn't seem to notice.

Kent had come to the beach to be alone. But even here, the boy got in the way. Kent didn't understand his sister's fascination with the human, or his father's obsession—they had been just fine on their own. Beachstone squatted down, sitting in the water and examining something beneath him. He sat. Kent watched.

No, Kent could hardly believe the accepted history that humans built the robots, that they had ruled the world, and Beachstone didn't help in convincing him. If Father was right that Beachstone was about the same age as Kent and Mary, one look made it apparent who should be the masters. He and his sister were the size of adult humans, and with more knowledge. All he saw in Beachstone was an inferior creature that could be crushed with ease. Humans died so easily. That was why there

25

were so few of them left. It was entirely plausible that something might happen to Beachstone on the beach right now, and that he might not return to Barren Cove alive. Like with the birds Kent liked to dissect, there was so little that separated human life from death.

Kent stood and walked down the beach. "What are you doing?" he said.

Beachstone stood and threw a shell into the approaching wave. It disappeared in the churning water.

"I guess you really think you're something, don't you?" Kent said. Beachstone continued to stare out at sea. "You're shit, you know that?" Kent said. He wanted the boy to look at him. "Father only brought you here because he felt sorry for you."

Beachstone looked at Kent. His pupils contracted; his eyes were steel. He started up the beach.

"Hey, come back here," Kent said. "Hey, come back; I'm just kidding. I'm just fooling around. You're not going to tell anybody, are you?"

Beachstone went into the cabana; Kent followed him. Beachstone went straight to the back room and closed the door. Kent had thought that humans were social creatures. Didn't they need companionship? Didn't they need to talk? Beachstone was less expressive than Kapec, and *he* predated complex emotions. The sound of water hitting water came from the back room, and Kent realized that Beachstone was urinating. He was fascinated despite himself. He had known what the bathrooms were for intellectually, but to see them used . . . He wished he had followed the boy so that he could witness it himself.

"Beachstone?" he called.

There was no answer. Kent had expected some of the humans from town to come looking for the boy almost as soon as he arrived, and so he had tried to have nothing to do with the human, because the human wasn't going to be there long. But when a week passed and they didn't come, Kent began to worry. His father and sister seemed to have reverted to slave robots, doting on the human's every need. Kent hated him. He hated him for taking away his family. He hated him for being special. But perhaps he was approaching it the wrong way. Perhaps he needed to invite the boy as an ally. He went to the cabinet where he kept his dissecting gear and pulled out the case along with a bird that he had cut open and tacked to a board.

Beachstone came out of the bathroom. Kent turned with the dead bird in hand, and the boy stopped and grimaced.

"I wanted to show you this. I found him on the beach. He was dead already, and something had picked at him; that's why there's blood on his feathers here." Kent set the board down on the table with the dissecting case next to it. Beachstone approached despite himself. "You see, that's his heart, and those are his lungs." Kent looked at Beachstone. "You've got those; that's what makes you breathe."

"I know that," Beachstone said.

"Okay, I'm sorry." At least he was talking, though. "You want to touch it?"

Beachstone reached out a hand and went right for the heart. He pulled back at the first touch and then dove in with both hands. "It smells like shit."

Kent opened his dissecting case. "Mary did that one with me. Because I found it already dead."

"She's got pretty hair," Beachstone said.

The comment renewed Kent's anger. He didn't have to make friends with this boy. He could kill him now. "Get up on the table," he said.

27

"Why?" Beachstone looked up at Kent, suspicious.

"I want to do an experiment. Come on—it'll be fun."

Beachstone put one foot on a chair, about to climb, when Kent reached below Beachstone's armpits and began to raise him. "Let go of me!" Beachstone started to wiggle. "Let go!"

"Okay, okay," Kent said, letting go. Beachstone was sitting on the table. "Lie down."

"What are you going to do?" Beachstone said.

"Just an experiment." Kent reached over and secured Beachstone's leg just below his shorts. Then he selected his sharpest scalpel from his dissecting kit. He moved fast, cutting into Beachstone's leg just above the knee, too fast for Beachstone to even move. Blood welled up around the cut immediately, and Kent could feel all the muscles in Beachstone's leg grow hard as the boy began to jerk away. Kent held him firmly though.

"Kent!" Mary yelled from the cabana doorway.

Beachstone knocked the dissecting box off the table, came up with another scalpel, and slashed across Kent's arm, cutting the simul-skin to the endoskeleton, and then Mary was on Kent. Her momentum knocked Kent to the ground, and she was able to secure him there, having caught him unawares. "What are you doing?"

"Just an experiment," Kent said, looking up at his sister. Her hair cascaded down either side of her face, making a tunnel that joined their two faces together in privacy.

"You were hurting him."

"Just an experiment."

"You can't hurt him."

"You helped before."

"Those were birds; this is different."

"Why?"

Mary's eyes looked like Beachstone's had on the beach: seething.

"Let me up."

"You can't hurt him. Father will deactivate you."

"Let me up, or I'll get up."

Mary let go.

Beachstone was still on the table, gripping his wound. Blood ran down the side of his leg and seeped out from between his fingers. He had remained silent through it all. He looked at Kent in defiance, refusing to give him the satisfaction of tears. Instead, a look of triumph crossed his face as he saw the sliced simul-skin on Kent's arm. Kent realized this and said, "But we don't bleed." Then he rushed out of the cabana.

Mary approached the table. "Let me see," she said.

Beachstone wouldn't let go.

"Let me see. I have to sew it up."

Beachstone opened his hands. The cut was deep, but it wasn't long.

"I'm impressed that you cut him back," Mary said, digging through the spilled contents of the dissecting box and finding a needle and thread. She held the needle in the flame of a lighter from the kit. "He didn't mean anything. He just likes to experiment."

"I'll tell Asimov 3000."

"Don't," Mary said, stopping for a second. "Please don't. He didn't mean anything."

Beachstone grabbed at his leg, and tears sprang to his eyes.

"Let me," Mary said, pushing Beachstone's hands away. She began to sew. Beachstone sucked air through his teeth. "It hurts," Mary said in amazement. "I'm sorry, I just forgot about it hurting."

"It's okay," Beachstone managed. "Just finish."

"Kent just needs lots of attention," Mary said as she worked. "He's not used to having to share our attention with somebody else. He's really harmless." Even through the pain, Beachstone didn't look as though he believed her. She realized his position and knew that what she was saying seemed thoughtless and insincere. She continued to sew in silence.

4.

SUNLIGHT FROM THE open window reflected on the dark mahogany dining room table, casting a white stripe down the center. Asimov 3000 dutifully waxed the wood once a year and dusted with a microfiber cloth once a week, so the table, which was never used, was as smooth as a mirror. Beachstone sat at the head of the table now. His collarbone was even with the tabletop, so he had to raise his arms at the shoulders in order to rest his hands on either side of the tablet sitting before him. Asimov 3000 had offered him a booster, but the boy refused, sitting on the edge of his seat and leaning forward to compensate for his height. The sun's reflection shone across the tablet as well, and the elderly robot could not be certain that the boy could even see the screen.

"Try again," Asimov 3000 said from the seat to the boy's left.

Beachstone tapped the screen, and a cheery female voice said, "B, buh, B. The boy has the ball."

"B, buh, B," Beachstone said after her.

"Don't just tap the screen for the answer," Asimov 3000 said. "Try it yourself."

"B, buh, B," Beachstone repeated.

"Try the next one without tapping for the answer first," Asimov 3000 said.

Beachstone touched the arrow to advance, and an animated worm rode a wagon to the center of the screen. The letter *W* appeared in uppercase and lowercase above the picture. "M, mommy, M," Beachstone said.

"It looks similar to an *M*," Asimov 3000 said, "but the *M*—"

"Q, qua, Q."

"Don't just guess," Asimov 3000 said.

Beachstone tapped the screen. The woman said, "W, wuh, W." Then he hit the next arrow.

How do I teach him patience? Asimov 3000 thought. The boy had identified all the letters and their sounds correctly only two days before. This was supposed to be review, and then they were going to work on sounding out three- and four-letter words. Asimov 3000 didn't know if the boy was getting the answers wrong deliberately in defiance for having been forced to sit down and work, or if the boy's biological mind was in some way lacking.

Beachstone scratched at his thigh for the fifth time.

"Is something bothering you there?" Asimov 3000 said. "Are you hurt?"

Beachstone brought his hand back up on the table. He tapped the next arrow and read, "F, fuh, F." He hit advance. "S, sss, S." His eyes flicked up to see how this sudden success was being received.

"Good," Asimov 3000 said. "Again."

The boy got the next one and the one after that. So his mistakes *had* been willful. It reminded Asimov 3000 of Master

Vandley's children. Then, *he* would sit at the head of the table with the children to either side of him—except on the days Master Vandley took charge of the children's lessons himself, of course—and sometimes the children would answer every question wrong for spite. But to get every question wrong, you had to know the right answers so as not to stumble upon them by accident.

Beachstone scratched his thigh again, but Asimov 3000 refrained from comment. He had not been distracted by his student's sudden improvement as the boy hoped, but if whatever Beachstone was hiding was important, it would come out. "Let's try some reading," he said. He took the tablet and navigated to the easy-reader section, then placed the tablet on the table in front of the boy.

" 'The c-aaa-t,' " Beachstone sounded out, " 'is ff-aaa-t.' " He took a deep breath, sat up straighter, and resumed. " 'The c-at is saaad.' "

"Good."

" 'The cat is aaa-lll-ss-ooo'— Alsoo?" Beachstone tapped the word, and the voice said, "Also." " 'Also.' Damn it."

"Don't give up so easily."

"I should have known that."

"Beachstone," Asimov 3000 said, and paused. The boy kept his eyes down. "You're learning. Try again."

" 'Also cr-cr-yuh.' " He reached to touch the screen, but Asimov 3000's hand darted out, blocking him.

"Try—"

Beachstone slid both hands under his teacher's, pressing the whole screen. The recordings for the rest of the words on the page all played at once over each other in a jumble of sound.

Asimov 3000 said nothing. They sat in silence for a moment, Beachstone with his head down.

"Why do I have to learn this stuff anyway?" Beachstone said.

"Why would you not want to learn to read?" Asimov 3000 said.

"Everything can read itself out loud. Or a robot can just do it for me."

"What if you need to read a sign? Or the power is out?"

"The power doesn't go out," Beachstone said.

"The power has not gone out in thirty-two point six four years, but it can happen."

Beachstone reached out and tapped the tablet. The woman's voice intoned, "Crying."

"This is a waste of time," Beachstone said. "I'm never going to need to read."

Asimov 3000 tried to think of a response. The boy's discouragement hurt. With Master Vandley's children, there was never any question as to what purpose learning to read served. Master Vandley presented it as an absolute fact. But Asimov 3000 had to admit that it had been seventy-three years since he'd last had a child pupil, and perhaps things had changed. "Try again," he said.

Beachstone didn't move.

Asimov 3000 considered. "There was a time when humans could trust robots, as you are suggesting, rely on them. But now, if you don't know how to read, you will never know who you can believe."

Beachstone's face pulled tight.

"You can't trust anyone anymore, Beachstone."

"What about you?" the boy said.

"Me, of course," Asimov 3000 said, "and your brother and sister—"

Beachstone flinched.

"Mary and Kent," Asimov 3000 corrected. "But you may not always wish to stay at Barren Cove." Master Vandley's children hadn't.

"I wish I could just upload reading into my brain like a robot," Beachstone said, and scratched his leg. "I wish I could just be a robot."

"You are so much more than a robot. Without you, there would be no me."

"There was 'you' long before there was me," Beachstone said.

"Without people," Asimov 3000 clarified.

"You were doing fine without me," Beachstone said.

No, I wasn't, Asimov 3000 thought. Mary and Kent had been consolation, but now there was purpose. "There is nothing more important than you," Asimov 3000 said. "I am here for *you*." He paused. "Okay?"

"So I should read for my protection?"

"Master Vandley read for pleasure as well. He told me he could read much faster than the tablet could talk."

"I'll read for protection," Beachstone said, and sat up and leaned forward. " 'The . . . cat . . . is also . . . crying.' " He advanced the page. " 'The ellff says, 'Do n-ah-t cry.' "

"Good," Asimov 3000 said.

Beachstone didn't reply. He shifted, bringing his legs up under him so he was on his knees, leaning over the table. Asimov 3000 resisted the impulse to reprimand the boy for having his feet on the chair. He did not want to discourage Beachstone now that he had resolved to work hard.

Beachstone continued to sound things out, the words that he had seen before coming faster and more fluidly, still scratching his leg at intervals.

The front door opened. The boy started at the sound,

watching the front hall through the dining room door. Kent appeared, paused, and went on.

Beachstone returned to his lesson, his focus uncanny, fending off any help Asimov 3000 tried to offer as he decoded the simple text and went on to the next story. The robot was proud that he had been able to instill such concentration, satisfied in a way that many robots today would not understand.

Eventually Asimov 3000 went to prepare a meal for the boy. The stripe of sunlight on the table had shifted, so it didn't quite reach the tablet anymore. The robot placed the plate on the table, but Beachstone didn't even glance at it. Asimov 3000's pride from earlier turned to worry. Such intensity could not be safe. Had he scared the boy too much with his talk of deceitful robots?

"'. . . break the egg,'" the boy read in an expressionless monotone.

"Good work," Asimov 3000 said.

The boy moved on to the next sentence.

5.

MARY STOOD AT the edge of the cliff behind the house watching the small speck on the beach below. From this distance, with no zoom, the boy looked like his namesake, like a stone that had been washed ashore. When she did zoom in, he came into focus, still as immobile as a rock, sitting with his feet flat in front of him so that his legs formed two triangles with the ground. His wrists resting on his knees, he held a tablet in front of his face. Good. He was safe. She checked on him every day at some point in the afternoon, worried that Kent would try something else to harm the boy.

Already as penitence, Mary had gone to town and found the small shop that served the human population. It brought in supplies on an as-needed basis, filling each human family's account of regularly ordered items—rice, flour, sugar, butchered meat. Mr. Brown, the shop owner, had been skeptical when Mary came into the store with her list of items. He asked if the order was to be charged to Mr. Vandley's account, that he thought Mr. Vandley had passed on, though the account hadn't been used in many years. But Mary set up a new account in her father's name and asked for it to be kept supplied regularly. The money she had slid across the counter had spurred Mr. Brown's attempt to fill the order.

But errands were the easy part. Mary wanted to interact with the boy directly again, like she had when she stitched him up. Father fawned over the boy, acting almost hostile to his own children, making it difficult for her to play a part in the human's care.

She watched the waves hurry up the beach, nearly touching Beachstone's feet, but stopping just short. Behind him, the cliff's shadow crept toward the water, poised to ensnare him, as though he sat in the light between two realms.

There had been moments when it seemed that Beachstone was pleased to see her. The way he relaxed when she came into whatever room he was in. She wished to message him at those times, but there was no way she could, and she didn't want to speak aloud in front of her father or brother. If only they had time alone.

She watched him some more. What was she afraid of? Hurting him? Being useless? Having misread his human cues? That he cared for her no more than he did for Kent? His manner when she had saved him from her brother had been anything but grateful. She reviewed every time they had been together. There was so little she understood.

There was only one way to learn.

She hurried to the beach stairs and didn't pause at the bottom, afraid to lose her momentum. She crossed through the cliff's shadow to the border of sun a few feet from the boy. Her shadow preceded her, and he looked back before she was alongside him.

"Hello," she said.

He squinted at her. "Move over one step. The sun's in my eyes."

She came around in front of him, on the wave-smoothed part of the sand, so the sun wouldn't be a concern. "Are you watching?" she asked.

He scratched his thigh. "I'm reading."

"Father taught you."

He turned back to the screen. She could see all the muscle movements in his face, the strain under his eyes above the cheekbone, a quivering millimeter at the left corner of his mouth, his ears pulled forward. His eyes were not following the words. He was uncomfortable and . . . angry. She *had* been wrong. He didn't care for her. "What are you reading?"

"Stories. About long ago when there were no robots, only people."

"Why?"

"Because they're exciting."

"Exciting like going to a carnival, or exciting like imminent danger?"

He looked at her, his eyes narrowed, and there was the hint of a smile at the corners of his mouth. Mary felt relieved. She hadn't realized quite how badly she needed him to like her. All those years of hearing her father speak of the Vandleys almost like gods. She wanted something like that for herself.

"I've never been to a carnival," he said at last.

"Neither have I," she said. "But I know of them."

"Sit down," Beachstone said. "I don't like you standing over me."

She complied, sitting cross-legged in front of him.

"Next to me," he said. "So we both can see the water."

She didn't understand why, but she did it anyway. He resumed reading without saying anything, scratching his leg occasionally. A sandpiper skittered to and fro, following the waves with precision. A group of gulls swooped at the water and then pulled up to land on the beach. Mary had seen these things before, but she studied them to avoid looking at Beachstone, knowing enough at least to know that staring made humans uncomfortable. After several minutes, Beachstone threw the tablet on the sand in front of them. Mary reached for it without thinking, and as she picked it up, she uploaded the story he had been reading.

It was about some kind of human with abilities no human ever possessed—flight, excessive strength, nearly instantaneous healing—as he fought a murderous cyborg.

"There was a cyborg—"

"He was defeated, but not deactivated," Mary said.

"You uploaded it?" Beachstone asked. His head flopped back in annoyance. "I was going to tell you the story." He grabbed the tablet and tossed it to his other side.

"You can still tell me," she said.

"No, I can't," he said, picking a seashell out of the sand.

She didn't understand why he was upset, only that he was. "Cyborgs never actually reached that level of technology," Mary said.

"And people never flew," Beachstone said. "It's a story."

"Entertainment."

They sat in silence for seventy-six seconds.

"Do you ever wonder?" Beachstone said.

"I predict. And worry about my predictions."

"It's not quite the same."

She figured it wasn't. But she didn't know how to do what he was asking. "Tell me a different story," she said.

"Forget it." He threw the shell toward the sandpiper. It fell short and the bird ignored it. He got onto his knees, and started pushing some of the dry sand into the wet sand. "Help me build a city," he said.

She crawled over to him and started to push more sand into his pile. He mixed the wet and the dry sand and started shaping it into a tower.

"I'll be the good guy," he said as he built. He examined her. "We'll both be good guys, but I'm more powerful. Start your own building."

She began a second pile. Beachstone was trying to smooth out his tower, so that it had flat sides, but it looked more like a skinny volcano. "Who is the bad guy?"

"We need better tools," he said, as a portion of his building sloughed off the side. He used that sand to start making another building, and then he looked at hers, which was wide, but had smooth sides in which she had used a shell to cut windows. "That's good," he said. "I could do better if I had some real tools."

Mary started another building next to her first. The idea of building a city meant just for them was challenging in a way that caused Mary's processors to come close to capacity. It was something she would never have considered.

"There's an evil robot who used to be a cyborg but ripped his last human parts out of him," Beachstone said. "Now he likes to cut apart humans like he did to his own body."

Mary felt a flicker of hurt at that scenario. She couldn't help but feel it implicated her brother and she felt protective, even if Kent's attack had made her livid. But at the same time, Beachstone had made her a good guy, and she didn't want to jeopardize that. She smoothed the conical top of her second building and began cutting a diamond pattern into it. When she noticed Beachstone had stopped digging, she looked up and saw he was watching her.

Suddenly, he knocked his first building over and then crushed another. He jumped up. "You don't think this is silly, do you?"

She wanted to say it was exciting, like the story he'd been reading, but she just shook her head no.

He looked up at the sky, then down the beach. Without another word he started running, away from the house. The cliff's shadow had overtaken the entire beach, and Mary worried he would be cold. She saw the discarded tablet, picked it up, and brought it into the cabana. Back on the beach, she zoomed and saw that he hadn't gone far. He was throwing something into the ocean. She didn't need to worry. Instead, as she mounted the stairs, she thought about building a city just for them.

• • •

Late the next afternoon, she found him on the beach, digging in the ruins of their city. She set down the bucket of tools she had brought him, from which he immediately drew a spade and continued working. "The cyborg's escaped," he said. "You say what happens next."

Mary knelt. What had been her buildings were now rounded lumps of wet sand, washed free of details by the ocean. A miniature tide pool had formed in the street Beachstone had built to connect them.

"The city suffers annual typhoons," Beachstone said, "and is in a constant state of being rebuilt."

"The cyborg escaped because the prison was damaged in the storm?" Mary said.

"Yeah," Beachstone said, a smile spreading across his face. "We've got to stop the cyborg, but all these people need our help too, because their homes have been destroyed."

"Do we each devote ourselves to one of the tasks for efficiency?" Mary asked.

"No, the people's immediate safety is most important. We need to build them shelters."

They set about doing that, building a complex of short, square buildings in a grid pattern. When they had twelve such buildings, indistinguishable from one another, Beachstone sat up. "Okay, that's enough," he said. He picked through the bucket of tools, pulled out a small rake, and dragged it through the sand at his side, making parallel tears that resembled freshly tilled farmland. His face was crunched in concern. "We need to drain the street," he said. He rifled through the tools some more and brought out a rusty trowel. He made a deep cut at the end of the tide pool, and the water started to flow toward the ocean.

"Now we find the cyborg?" Mary asked.

"Now we find the cyborg," Beachstone said.

Mary waited for him to say something else, but he didn't. "Where is he?" she said.

"I don't know. Where would you go?"

She looked at the world they had just completed. "Tunnel under the new shelters. Destabilize the foundations. Let the whole thing collapse."

Beachstone grinned. "That would kill hundreds of people. Perfect."

Mary felt a wave of happiness. She had contributed to the story and he had liked it! She cast her eyes down and smiled.

"You start at that end, and I'll—" He broke off, staring at her. He reached out with his sand-covered hand as though he was going to touch her face. "You look . . ."

She turned her head away, embarrassed. Had she done something wrong? Then how come she could feel her smile broaden? She checked his expression. Now he looked down, bashful.

He started digging on his side of the shelters. "You dig on that side, and I'll dig on this side, and we'll see if we can meet in the middle without it falling apart."

Mary picked out another trowel. Digging with her hands was causing small abrasions in the simul-flesh on her fingertips, making them rough.

They worked in silence, pausing on occasion to check the other's progress. The sand, black flecked, became more and more difficult to bore through, packed hard. The cliff's shadow was upon them, and the holes were as dark as night. Mary saw the sweat running down Beachstone's face. "Are you all right?" she said.

He sat back on his heels. "I'm fine," he said, but he was pale as well as sweaty. "We need to dig a moat, so the tunnel doesn't fill with water. We're not going to finish it today." He stood up and ran his trowel in a straight line between the complex and the ocean, cutting deeper and deeper. Mary moved over to help. When Beachstone judged their work sufficient, he threw the trowel aside and lay down on the sand, looking up at the darkening sky. He rested his hands on his stomach and gave a deep sigh. "Thank you," he said.

Mary was confused. He was thanking her? She made the appropriate reply. "You are welcome."

A land breeze passed over them toward the sea, and Beachstone sat up. "I'm hungry," he said. He stood and shook the sand off his clothes. "Make sure to put the tools in the cabana so they don't get washed away." He started for the cliff stairs.

Mary watched him go and then collected the tools.

• • •

It was a week and a half after they began building—almost three weeks since the incident in the cabana—when Mary realized she had never removed Beachstone's stitches. They worked on their city every afternoon now, after Beachstone's morning lessons with her father. Sometimes Mary waited for him on the beach, and sometimes she joined him after he had already settled down with his reading tablet. They never descended the stone stairs together, and neither ever worked on the city without the other.

That day, Beachstone was already at the beach when she arrived. When he saw her shadow approach, he turned, his sudden smile suffusing his whole demeanor. "Hey, sidekick," he said.

"Hey, hero," she answered. Every smile she elicited from the boy felt like a surge of energy flooding her core.

He set down his tablet, scratching his leg, something that had become a subconscious habit with him. "Where were we?" he said.

Mary held up the first aid kit she had brought with her. "How would you like to get those stitches out?"

His smile fell and his eyes narrowed.

"It shouldn't hurt," Mary said.

"How would you know?"

It was true. She couldn't.

Beachstone stood, sand falling away from his pants. "Okay," he said. "In the cabana." He started up the beach, expecting her to follow.

The success of their first tunnel had inspired Beachstone to construct a complete underground system below their city. They had added a seawall to the moat, but water still ended up in the tunnels, so each day began with bailing, which Beachstone merely worked into the story. Imagination still perplexed Mary. She tried to find patterns in the narrative connections he made, and ventured occasional contributions. He seemed to like everything that she had done so far, but she also wanted his criticisms; how else would she learn without input from past experiences to better inform future actions? But there had to be a first term, she figured. At least the stitches were an objective task she could complete.

In the cabana, Beachstone removed his pants and jumped up on the table in the same place she had stitched him up. His legs were shockingly white in comparison to his sun-browned arms and face. The cut on his thigh was pale pink except at the top, where it was raised and reddish, the black sutures like a line of ants.

She brought out the rubbing alcohol, which had to be decades old, the plastic bottle milky yellow with age. She opened a sterile swab and used it to wash the wound, and then wiped the surgical scissors and tweezers as well before using the tweezers to grab the knot at the end of the stitches.

Beachstone watched with a fascination that reminded Mary of Kent at his dissections. Her brother had created an experiment, after all. She cut the knot off and used the tweezers to gently pull the thread through the skin, which stretched before relinquishing the suture. "Did it hurt?" she asked.

"No," he said.

She moved to the next one, and a small dot of blood appeared where the thread pulled through. She touched the alcohol swab to it, and Beachstone's leg jerked. "Sorry," she said.

"It was just cold," he said.

She pulled the rest of the stitches out, and there was some blood, but not much until she reached the red, raised section at the top. When she pulled the thread out there, there was some pus as well as heavier bleeding, almost as though the cut had reopened just there. She blotted away the blood, but when she took away the gauze, more blood welled up, so she covered it and applied pressure.

Beachstone drew a sharp breath through his teeth.

She checked his expression. His face was pinched, and he was sweating. "Are you okay?" she said.

"I'm fine," he said, pushing her hand away. "It's just a little blood." He jumped off the table, and the blood began to drip down his leg.

"Cover it," she said.

He took the gauze and held it to the wound. "Come on," he said. "Let's build."

Mary was unsure. She did not like the way the wound was bleeding. It should have been fully healed by now.

As usual, Beachstone didn't wait for her. He picked up his pants and headed down the beach, partially bent over and limping as he tried to keep pressure on the cut. When he got to the city, he knelt and grabbed a ladle they used for bailing and began to empty one of the tunnels, letting go of his wound.

Mary wondered if a time would come when she would ever understand this creature. She thought the answer was no, and that thrilled and troubled her at the same time. All she could do was collect data. She closed up the first aid kit and left it in the cabana as she rejoined the boy.

• • •

That night, Asimov 3000 stopped outside the open door to Mary's room after putting Beachstone to bed.

"Mary?" her father called. She stepped into view from her place behind the door. "Ah, Mary," he said at the sight of her. "I cannot express enough how much joy it gives me to see you take to Beachstone as you have."

Mary thought of her time with the boy, the intimacy. It wasn't something you could ever have with another robot. She could hardly comprehend what her life had been before Beach-stone had come to Barren Cove.

"I cannot express my own joy," Mary said.

"Your brother worries me though."

Mary had a moment of panic. They had all contrived to keep the incident in the cabana a secret from her father.

"He seems distant, absent. Has he spoken to you?"

Mary shook her head. "No."

"I want all three of you to get along, to become fast friends."

No! Mary thought, Our city is ours alone! But then she felt guilty, because she knew that, as much as her brother had retreated, it was in part because she had abandoned him. "Yes, Father."

"You are all my children," Asimov 3000 said.

She knew what Kent's reaction to that would be, and Beach-stone's, and even she couldn't succumb to this fallacy. "I will speak to him," she said.

"Because I never could have hoped . . ."

"What, Father?"

"Nothing."

She couldn't guess what he had been going to say. She was too distracted with her sudden need to protect what she and Beachstone had forged.

Asimov 3000 put his hand on her shoulder and squeezed. "You're doing so well," he said.

"Thank you."

"I love you," he messaged.

"I love you too," she returned.

Asimov 3000 withdrew his hand. He gave a single nod of his head and continued down the passage into the dark.

Despite her defensiveness, the conversation did make her wonder about Kent. They had always spent time together during the day, following whatever mechanical or biological fancy had captured her brother's attention. He must be lonely. But she couldn't get past the idea that she didn't want him anywhere near Beachstone. And, with even more guilt, she found that she didn't really miss Kent's exploits.

When, hours later, she heard her brother come in and go into his room beside hers, she tried to work up the desire to speak with him. She had told her father she would. But she was afraid of what might come from the conversation—her brother's vitriol, or his misunderstanding that she was inviting him to enter her and Beachstone's world.

Instead, she powered down for the night.

6.

KENT SAT ASTRIDE his dirt bike, waiting for the engine to heat up after the oil change he'd just completed. He had taken the bike apart and rebuilt it three times in the past month and was growing bored with it. It was time to send for some real motorcycles. He would love to take an antique gasoline model and convert it to solar electricity—a true challenge given the bike's limited surface area—but he would settle for a modern electric to start. It would take long enough to get a common model to Barren Cove, and he needed something to distract himself lest his bitterness over Beachstone require a more drastic outlet than the small pranks he visited on the boy—waking him repeatedly in the middle of the night, locking him out of all the bathrooms, shoving, tripping, pinching at every opportunity. Watching the boy flinch at his approach was fun, but he wanted to draw blood again. It was only the risk of his father's ire that held him back.

And then there was Mary.

Mary, who no longer seemed to know he existed. Who preferred to play with her pet human, to fawn over him; the way she debased herself before him. To abandon her only brother! He revved the engine of his bike. He'd seen the two of them playing in the sand in the afternoons. It was another beautiful day. Perhaps he'd join them.

He released the kickstand and took off, pushing the bike to the limit. The speed only fed his rage; the memory of Mary on top of him in the cabana, holding him down. He wanted to kill the boy.

He reached the spot where the cliff was low enough that he could attempt a jump to the beach. The sand was horrible for the bike, he knew, but he didn't care; it would give him a challenge when he next did maintenance. He flew off the edge, the flat ocean stretching before him like an endless road, and then the bike skidded in the sand, spun, and Kent found himself on the ground, one leg pinned beneath the machine. Without pause, he righted the bike and forced it down the beach toward the water, until the rattle of the sand crunching against the motor fell away, and he was on the hard-packed beach at the water's edge, the waves spraying to either side of the bike like walls of water.

He zoomed his vision and could make out the speck of Beachstone in the distance. He seemed to be alone. Kent grinned. A wave skittered up, the water splashing beneath his tires, and Kent was curious to see how his brake pads would work.

As he approached Beachstone, Kent saw that the boy was reading from a tablet resting on his crossed legs. He didn't look up, even when he must have been able to hear the buzz of the motor. When he was only feet away, Kent executed a spinning stop, spraying Beachstone with sand. The boy cringed, raising his hands in front of his face as though to ward off a blow.

Kent jumped off the bike, letting it fall to the ground, the engine still running, and he grabbed Beachstone's tablet before the boy had a chance to block him. He looked at the screen. "Ah, superheroes," he said. "You humans did like to dream you could be better than you really are." He threw the tablet into the ocean like it was a Frisbee, the dark, spinning rectangle traveling a good sixty or seventy yards before falling into the water.

He circled the seated boy, whose nose and lips trembled in rage, even as he drew in his shoulders in order to make himself small. Kent smirked. He saw the little mounds of sand that spread out covering almost ten square feet, holes at various points; he guessed they were meant to be buildings. He kicked the one closest to him, the sand spraying over the others.

"Hey," Beachstone said, starting to get up, but Kent turned on the boy, and Beachstone sat back down, ducking.

"Where's your servant?" Kent said. "You need me to get anything? Somehow, you lost your tablet."

"She's not my servant; she's my sidek—" He bit his lip.

"Your sidek . . . ? Your sidekick. I see. And you must be a superhero, then." Kent faked as though he were going to strike the boy, and Beachstone flinched. Kent grinned. This was fun. Maybe he could see why Mary would want to spend time with the bastard. He bent down so he was close to Beachstone's face. "Do you feel super now?"

Beachstone gritted his teeth and averted his eyes.

"Can you pull me apart with your bare hands? Because I could you."

"Shut up," Beachstone said.

Kent noticed some blood soaking through Beachstone's pants. He grabbed the boy's leg—

"Hey! Stop!"

—straightened it, knocking the boy into a lying position, and pulled up the leg of Beachstone's pants.

The boy was hitting at him, jerking away.

"Ooo," Kent said. "That doesn't look good." Part of the scalpel cut seemed to have healed, but the skin around the top was bright candy-apple red.

"Kent!"

Kent jerked. Mary was half running, half walking toward them from the cliff stairs. As much as he wanted to hurt Mary, to make her pay for leaving him, he felt panic at her finding him laying hands on Beachstone again. He let go of the boy, who remained lying down. "Ah, Mary," Kent said, grinning. "Our hero."

She was walking now, watching him with suspicion. She stopped a few feet away.

"Or, no," Kent said, backing away from the boy, "what was it? Our 'sidekick.'"

For each step Kent took back, Mary took a step closer.

"Shut up," Beachstone said, sitting up.

"You hear how he talks?" Kent said. "Does he order you around too?"

Mary was beside Beachstone now, but she never took her eyes off her brother.

"Your human is sick," Kent said. Beachstone was pale and sweating profusely, his breathing coming in short gasps.

"What's wrong with you?" Mary said.

At that, Kent's rage blossomed, his eyes growing wide. "What's wrong with *me*?" he said. "With *me*? What happened to you and to Father? What's wrong with the two of you, losing yourselves to this . . ." He kicked sand at Beachstone, who turned his head away. "This anachronism."

"Haven't you noticed how happy Father is?" Mary said.

"When would I have noticed? He doesn't have time for us anymore."

"You're the one off playing with your bikes," Mary said.

"No, you're right," Beachstone said suddenly, managing a sly smile. "He doesn't care about you anymore. Now he's got me."

Kent moved toward Beachstone, and Mary took a step forward, and then Kent yelled at the sky, a groan of angry frustration. "He's an arrogant, self-serving pissant. You know he doesn't think of us as anything more than machines."

"No," Mary said. "That's what he makes *you* feel."

Beachstone rolled over and vomited a goopy yellow liquid. Mary bent down to him.

"Weak," Kent said. "All of us. Weak."

Beachstone wiped his mouth with the back of his hand and sat back up.

"Go away, Kent," Mary said, squatting beside the boy. "You've had your fun."

And that's it, Kent thought. A dismissal. I'm no more than an annoyance. Me! Her own brother. But she loves this animal more. "We'll see if you're saying that in eighty years, when your beloved here is a corpse, and you're all alone." He went to his bike and righted it. It had stalled out. He straddled it and restarted its engine. "And all of this," Kent said, gesturing with his head to indicate their sand constructions. He gunned the bike, passing only inches from Beachstone and Mary, plowing into the sand buildings and mounds, when suddenly his bike flipped up and he flew over the handlebars.

Mary wanted to rush to her brother, the way she had to Beachstone when the boy had been sick only moments before, but for some reason she stayed still. Beachstone was on his feet, all his weight on his good leg, his face flushed.

Kent got up and stomped to his bike. The tunnels under a

huge section of the city had collapsed under his weight, forming the pothole that had flipped the bike. Kent dragged it from the hole, his jaw set in embarrassment. He wouldn't look like a fool. He mounted and looked at them. He could see in Mary's face utter repugnance, as though she had ceased to love him in that very moment. "Enjoy your little sand castles," he said.

Mary shook her head.

Beachstone limped forward, his eyes boring into Kent. "I won't always be smaller than you," Beachstone said.

Kent revved his engine. "But you'll always be weaker." And he drove away.

7.

BEACHSTONE FELL ILL the next day with a high fever. During the following week, he lay in bed drifting in and out of sleep while Asimov 3000 kept watch day and night. The human's sickness—his mere presence—had a way of becoming the center of life at Barren Cove. Mary made frequent trips to Mr. Brown's, inventing errands just to feel useful. Her father wouldn't let her do anything with his patient firsthand, and her separation from the boy made her anxious. Did her father blame her for Beachstone's sickness?

The weather turned against them as well, the sky a dusty white with no sun for days, making the sickroom perpetually dark and damp. The sporadic rain, lurching from a palpable mist to a torrent, never ceasing, melted away their city on the beach below, the only remnant of their fantasy world the pool that formed in the cave-in caused by Kent's bike.

On the day that Asimov 3000 decided that Beachstone was well, Mary checked the bread in the oven. It had risen and spread out above the rim of the metal pan. What was visible was now a light golden brown. She hoped that it was right. She referenced the image in a cookbook and it seemed to match. She had never seen bread before—it was not a commodity Mr. Brown could procure—but she had followed the recipe exactly. It had to be right. She took the pan from the oven and set it out to cool.

She prepared the inside of the sandwich next, laying three slices of turkey on the counter, topping them with a slice of Swiss cheese, and spreading a daub of mustard atop it. The sandwich construction was so utilitarian; it was ingenious, really. Bread, meat, bread—it was clean, required no utensils to eat, and was nutritious. She hoped that Beachstone would like it. She just wanted to make him happy.

She sliced the loaf, finished the sandwich, and packed it in a paper bag. Now they could stay out for most of the day. Beachstone would have food; they wouldn't have to return home.

Mary took the lunch and went upstairs. Her father sat beside the bed; Beachstone had still not gotten up. "Don't you want to go out?" Mary asked. "The sun has finally arrived."

Beachstone looked at Asimov 3000. The robot nodded, and Beachstone jumped out of the bed. He almost tripped when his bad leg hit the ground, but he readjusted, and he managed to make the limp seem part of a game.

"Don't tax him," Asimov 3000 said.

"I made you lunch," Mary said to Beachstone.

"You carry it," Beachstone said, going out ahead of her.

As Mary passed Kent's room, he messaged, "Going to rebuild your sand lumps?"

She stopped in his doorway. He had his back to her as he tinkered with a toy car engine in pieces on his desk. "I thought I'd take him to town," Mary said. "You want to come?"

Kent turned, his hands still putting the engine together. "No, but good luck with that."

"What's that supposed to mean?"

"Your superhero will never make it."

"Mary, come on," Beachstone called from halfway down the stairs.

Kent turned back to the almost completed engine. "You better go. The human calls." As soon as the engine was complete, Kent began to disassemble it again.

Mary wanted to say something, but she couldn't think of anything else to say. She turned and joined Beachstone at the bottom of the stairs.

• • •

Outside, Beachstone's limp was more obvious, but since he didn't say anything about it, Mary let him be. They went down the cliff stairs to the beach and, without a glance at their city in ruins, walked toward town in silence. A constant breeze from the shore enveloped them, shaping to the contours of their bodies. The breeze made Mary realize how hot it was in the sun. She knew how the heat affected Beachstone, and noticed the slight shimmer of moisture on his forehead, but that didn't seem to be what bothered him. His jaw was clenched and his brow was down. He was angry, but she didn't know why.

The beach was strewn with seaweed in parallel trails that led to the water. The occasional discarded shell of a horseshoe crab marked their distance. Mary zoomed in and saw the town up ahead.

They trudged forward as though on a mission as opposed to a promenade. Beachstone was going so fast that his hands jerked up for balance with each limp. Mary finally stopped. "Beachstone, what is it?"

He turned on her, with almost the same expression he had

thrown at Kent when the tunnels collapsed. "You invited him to come," he said.

She had never been the subject of such wrath, and it cut her, her processors recycling so she stammered, "I knew he wouldn't. Father—"

"Don't ever invite him again. It's him or me. Always."

She was too overcome, her system freezing several seconds before she was able to whisper, "I'm sorry."

His sneer softened, and an element of guilt seeped into his expression. "Never," he said. "I cannot be near him ever."

"Okay. All right," she said. His words panicked Mary. He's changed, she thought. Though Father might have blamed her for Beachstone's illness, there was no question of where Beachstone assigned fault. But he was angry at her? If only he would smile.

He looked away, and after a moment said, "Let's go swimming." He ran ahead into the water. "Ow, it hurts, it hurts, it hurts."

Mary rushed to him, holding the lunch bag above her head. "Are you okay?"

"The water burns my cut," he said, squatting down, smiling now. "Leave the lunch on the beach." Mary started for the beach. "Just throw it." The bag skidded on the wet sand. Mary walked through the water to where Beachstone was treading, unsure if he even wanted her. "Come here," he said, and his expression was a familiar one. He hadn't changed; he'd just been angry.

She went to him, and he latched onto her back. They had never been swimming before, always keeping to dry land. The excitement and Beachstone's suddenly light tone helped to ease some of the anxious pain from moments before. *This* was what she had missed, this . . . spontaneity. She continued forward, pulling him out into the water, and found herself, as always, wishing she could be like him, wishing she could have the same impulsive manner. She decided to try. "You on tight?" she asked, excited by the uncertainty.

"Yeah," he said.

Mary dove, spinning around, and then brought him back up.

He beat at her, laughing and choking. "Monster," he said. He pulled himself around so that he was in front of her.

"What?" she said, playing innocent, relieved at his laughter.

"What!" he said.

"What?" she said, and then smiled.

He tried to dunk her but couldn't. He settled, his legs around her torso. "Your hair's wet," he said.

"So's yours," Mary said.

He picked up a strand of her hair. "What's it made out of?"

"It's real hair. Human, I mean."

He twisted it around his finger, but it slid away from him. He grabbed at it again. Mary watched him examine her lock of hair. His eyes were intent, his brow furrowed. There was the sound of a distant motor, and Beachstone looked up. "We should keep moving," he said.

"There's no hurry."

He detached himself from her and started swimming toward the shore.

"Wait. There's no hurry." Mary caught up with him. They were walking now, emerging from the water, the sand shifting beneath their feet. Mary noticed a cut on the back of Beachstone's arm, a fine line that ended in a deep red dot. "Wait, you're cut. Let me see," Mary said, grabbing for him. Beachstone fought in her arms. "Let me see."

"No," he said, pushing her hands away.

She held his arms down and looked over his shoulder at the

back of his arm. The bleeding had already stopped. The cut was superficial. "It's nothing," Mary said. She let go of him. She thought of Kent's parting barb from weeks ago: that robots don't bleed. Organic life was so fragile.

Beachstone grabbed ahold of her and squeezed, and Mary had a sudden understanding of what a hug was for. She gripped him back, restraining herself from crushing him. There was always so much to learn. So many things that she knew but did not understand. When Beachstone let go, Mary expected to see tears on his face, but there were none. Instead his eyes were set in a look of determination. Again, Mary was thrown by how little she understood his human emotions. Perhaps they functioned differently in a biomass than they did in herself. Beachstone turned toward town, and they walked. "Have you ever been to town?" Mary asked.

"I don't know," he said.

He didn't say anything more.

The sun had reached its apex. "Do you want your sandwich?"

"No," Beachstone said without looking at her.

The cliff began to drop away. The rate of its decline seemed to match the sun's descent so that it appeared as if the sun wasn't moving at all. Mary noticed that Beachstone's limp had become more pronounced even as their pace slowed; he was in pain. Mary wondered what the pain felt like. She had never been damaged. Sometimes her systems didn't run as quickly as she was used to, or she realized that she was frozen, unable to complete a motion, but she was always able to fix the problem by running diagnostics or rebooting her system. It was nothing more than being tired or overworked, a software glitch. But Beachstone's software was working with no problem. She could tell by the set of his face, so resolute.

"Is your leg all right?" she asked.

"I'm fine," he said.

Mary looked for any sign of strain in his face. There was none. She knew from his week of convalescence that he needed to eat, he needed to drink—she hadn't brought water! "Maybe we should turn back."

He stopped, and looked out at the ocean.

"What?" Mary said.

"I think I'll have lunch now," he said. He held out his hand for the bag. Relieved, Mary put it in his hand. He sat, crossing his good leg under his body, allowing the injured leg to flop on the beach. Mary sat beside him, trying to judge how close she should be. "We're not going back," Beachstone said with food in his mouth.

"I don't want you to get sick again," she said.

"I'm fine."

"I really think we should go back," Mary said.

"We're not going back," he repeated, now with a tinge of his anger from earlier.

It frightened her, but so did the way Beachstone was sweating. She looked up at the sun. "We didn't bring any water," she said.

"I heard Kent. First you invited him, then he mocked me. I won't let him gloat. We're going to make it."

"We could say we made it."

"No," Beachstone said, and settled on chewing.

Mary worried one of the rough spots on her hands. "Was the sandwich good?" she asked.

Beachstone pulled himself closer to her. He reached for Mary's hair; it had dried in the sun. She felt him brush his fingers along the bottom. She wanted to touch his hair too. Could it be that it really grew from his head? Could it be that he would have to cut it? She reached out and touched it. It was just like hers.

"We better go," Beachstone said, jumping up.

Mary was confused. She felt cheated. He was so angry one moment, then affectionate, and then distant the next. It made it hard for her to sort out her own feelings. Could it be that her brother felt the same way about the boy, and that was why he had wanted to hurt him? She was surprised to find that she could understand this—her own feelings of, what? Love? She felt as though she wanted to be beside him always, to appease him, to ease him, to serve him, and yet, it was crushing. Was it only two months ago that Father had brought him home? What had she done with herself before then?

She had to run to catch up with him.

Beachstone's limp was better after the rest, but it gradually returned as they walked. He had slackened his pace again without noticing. "I could carry you," Mary said when they stopped for a moment so that Beachstone could stretch.

"I'm fine," he said.

Mary wanted to think of something that could make him laugh. She looked at the cliff face. It would be easy to scale it. Maybe she could carry him on her back and they could walk up above where the ground was solid. Perhaps the sand was hard on his feet as it slid away from beneath each step. But she didn't say anything. They walked. When they rested, they leaned together, Beachstone's arm held lightly around Mary's waist. Beachstone didn't seem as intent as before, but he didn't deviate from his path. At one point he smiled suddenly, and Mary looked up to try and see what had made him happy. She didn't see anything. It was only much later that she realized that was the moment when his human eyes could perceive the town for the first time. The cliff was little more than a steep incline now. It was dusk.

They reached the town after dark. Beachstone was silent.

His head dropped forward, but Mary realized too late what was happening, and he was on the ground in front of her before she could move to grab him. Stupid kid, he had pushed himself too far. Mary was angry with her brother just then. She watched Beachstone's inert form for a moment. He had sprawled into such an unnatural position—and yet, it was supremely natural, for it had happened, hadn't it, and happened only as it could have. Then she bent down and picked him up. She knew she needed to get him a drink, but all the lights in town were out; there was no one on the street. She walked through the empty streets, carrying Beachstone in front of her. She had never been in town at night, and it was all new to her. They were the buildings she knew, but without the people they were different. The stillness seemed appropriate, and she was glad that Beachstone wasn't missing the town she knew, and yet she was upset that this new town, which she was seeing for the first time, couldn't be shared with him. When she found nobody, she decided that there was nothing to do but to return home. He would sleep now. He could drink at home.

She walked out of town, choosing the high ground for the return.

8.

ASIMOV 3000 WATCHED over the boy. He hadn't reset the night before, and he was afraid to reset now. He was afraid to leave the boy's side. What had his daughter been thinking? Couldn't she see how pale the boy was? He stood up and crossed the room. The day's early light streamed through the lace curtains, casting the room in an opal glow. It didn't seem fitting for the gravity of the sickbed. He would bring the boy water. He would wake him, force the liquid into him. She hadn't brought water!

At the door, Asimov 3000 turned back and looked at the small form sleeping in the bed. Master Vandley had laid in that bed, also shrunken, his biological children long since gone, first from his house, then from this life, victims of the plague that had never reached Barren Cove. And yet, what difference had that made? Master Vandley had been so sick anyway—hours upon hours Asimov 3000 had watched over his body. Yes, he knew how to take care of a sick human. The fresh bread that Mary had made yesterday morning had fooled him, made him trust her, causing him to forget—his own children didn't know humans. He couldn't blame her.

The water. He was afraid to leave. Surely it would be fine for just a moment.

He went down the hall. As he passed Mary's room, he looked in to find her sitting in her chair in front of the vanity. She was asleep, though. Kent called from his room. "Father?"

"I'm getting water," Asimov 3000 answered as he passed by, and went downstairs without looking in on his son. In the kitchen, Asimov 3000's system froze just inside the swinging door, paralyzing him for a moment. He needed to go forward, to go forward, to go forward, and yet he was riveted to the floor. Take a step, he thought. Water. Take a step. But his system remained frozen. And then he was walking across the room to the cabinet. He filled a glass with water and headed back upstairs.

Beachstone hadn't moved. Asimov 3000 set the glass of water on the nightstand beside the bed and then took up his seat. He hadn't just skipped rebooting the night before. He hadn't rebooted the whole week of Beachstone's illness. The freeze in the kitchen—he should sleep. "Beachstone," he said.

The boy slept on.

Master Vandley had had so much to say, even in the end. "It is only fitting," he had said so often. It was only fitting that Asimov 3000 have Barren Cove. It was only fitting that male and female robots have different programming, a new development at that time. "You'll be one of the last that can procreate asexually," Master Vandley had said. The last time Asimov 3000 had been to town he had felt out of place even among the robots.

Master Vandley had been right. When Asimov 3000 built Kent and then Mary, he encoded them each with a discrete sex. It was only fitting, then, that he didn't understand them any better than they understood their new brother. Beachstone didn't know why he had been left on the beach or by whom, or at least that was what he claimed, and so Asimov 3000 didn't know either, but he knew that he was meant to bring the boy home. He knew that there needed to be a human in Master Vandley's bed again. He knew that Kent had cut the boy. And he worried about that.

But Mary had taken to the boy like, well, like a human, like the way Master Vandley's daughter had taken to the town boy. But Mary had still hurt him—no water! He tried to wake Beachstone again. He had to.

He stood and shook the boy. Beachstone mumbled in his sleep, shrugged away from Asimov 3000, and then opened his eyes. "You need to drink," Asimov 3000 said, holding up the glass.

Beachstone took it and brought it to his lips. He began to gulp.

"Slowly."

Beachstone stopped, coughing, then belched, and then started drinking again, watching Asimov 3000 with big eyes.

Perhaps he needed to worry that Mary had taken to the boy so closely as well. When Beachstone finished, he took the glass. "How do you feel?"

"We made it to the town," Beachstone said, breaking into a large smile.

"What were you thinking?" Asimov 3000 asked.

"Nobody was awake," the boy said, and then went back to sleep.

Asimov 3000 sat down. I should go fill the glass again, he thought. He didn't get up. I should sleep. But he watched the boy breathe instead. His chest rose and fell, a deep intake, a short burst out through the nose. Rose and fell. Asimov 3000's own children breathed. It was another robot innovation, a clever illusion that the humans hadn't thought to include and that robots had taken on themselves. A slight rise and fall of the chest at the right time, and we were oh so human.

He would have to explain to Mary how delicate Beachstone was, although he thought that yesterday would be enough of a lesson. I would have thought last week would have been enough of a lesson, but I guess I would have been wrong. No, yesterday was enough of a lesson.

Asimov 3000 realized that he had not leaned back when he intended to lean back. He tried again. He couldn't. Tried again. Leaned back too hard, as all three commands acted at once. He kicked out his legs to prevent the chair from tipping back.

Master Vandley had had a human from town come and take care of the new will. The human had brought an assistant to act as a witness. Asimov 3000 was a permissible second witness. The will had been unnecessary, but Master Vandley had been a businessman, and he liked his business tidy. Barren Cove was Asimov 3000's. Its clean running water, which had been unused for five years, was Asimov 3000's.

Beachstone breathed.

Asimov 3000 would have liked to see him grow up. But that also meant seeing him grow old. I should reboot, Asimov 3000 thought. I should sleep. And yet, perhaps it was only fitting if the children took over. At least they would have known a human.

9.

"OPENING CLOSETS?"

I looked up to see Clarke stepping into the cabana, and then, before I could answer him, the bicycle girl appeared behind him. Flustered, I turned my head every which way, scanning around me as though I had lost something, avoiding seeing them.

Dean shut off her recording. The sound of the ocean filled the sudden silence.

Clarke sat at the table and kicked his legs up. "That's the past, Sapien. Old news. Time to live in the now."

The bicycle girl circled in place, spinning only one wheel while keeping the other stationary. I watched her as she surveyed the room. "Can I help you?" I said.

Clarke's momentum was thrown off by the question. He must have planned his entrance but hadn't thought beyond that, let alone what to do if I actually answered. He took his legs down and leaned on the table. "That's Jenny," he said. "Jenny, Sapien."

Jenny turned and looked at me. "Hi," she said. I hid my damaged hand under the table. Aside from the bicycle wheels and the pink hair, she appeared normal in every way. Clarke was much more monstrous. I tried to catch her eye, but she was looking at something on the floor that I couldn't see because Clarke was in the way. Besides, I had seen the floor many times; it was just tile.

"Sapien!" Clarke said, drawing my attention. He hadn't anticipated the effect Jenny would have on me. He wanted me disconcerted, but he wanted me to listen to him. "We came to invite you to party."

"Party?"

He pulled out some memory chips from his pocket and tossed them on the table. They clinked against the glass. "We're gonna get fucked up, you know? Go into town. Meet some of our friends." He jumped up, standing on the chair. "Party!"

Jenny came around the table. She seemed to float. She put her hand on my shoulder and slid it across to the other shoulder as she wheeled behind me. She leaned down, her hair brushing the side of my face. Pink, I thought. "Come on," she said. "It'll be fun."

Clarke raised his head, screamed, and jumped onto the built-in cabinet that lined one of the walls yelling, "Party!"

"I promise," Jenny said in my ear.

Clarke jumped onto Jenny's back. She was unprepared for the weight and our heads knocked. By the time I looked up she had wheeled around in front of me. She moved so fast. She wheeled back and forth in place with Clarke riding her piggyback. "Grab the sims, robo; let's go."

I looked at the chips on the table. I had been comfortable learning about my neighbors from Dean without actually interacting with them. But Clarke was right in front of me now.

Where did he come in? Why would he want to party with an old robot like me? I could easily see us getting to town and, the joke's on me, he had promised his friends a bit of fun with the old robot living in his "beach house." I remembered him tossing my new arm off the cliff and catching it again and again.

Clarke slapped Jenny's ass. "Yah!" he yelled. "Yah!" He leaned forward. Jenny zoomed out onto the beach. Her wheels kicked up a spray of sand behind her.

She had touched me. Her hair had brushed against my cheek. She had promised me a good time. Wasn't this why I had left the city? Maybe I just needed to have some fun. Jenny and Clarke pulled doughnuts in the sand. I grabbed the memory chips from the table, put them in a pocket, and went outside.

Jenny pulled up to me, and Clarke jumped off. He played his trademark sound bite: "Ha, ha, ha, ha, ha." Then he turned to go. Jenny followed, and I followed behind.

The night was clear. The moon, near full, reflected on the ocean. At the top of the cliff, there was a yellow motorcycle. Clarke climbed aboard. "You need to get wheels, humanoid," Jenny said.

"I've got wheels," Clarke said, and he revved the motorcycle. "Hand me one of those chips," he said to me.

I reached into my pocket, still afraid that Clarke would turn on me at any moment.

"What about the others?" Jenny said.

"Fuck the others. Preparty." I pulled the chips out. Clarke grabbed one and shoved it into the USB port on his chest. "Come on, come on."

Jenny held her hand out and I handed her a chip. She uploaded it.

"I have never—" I started.

Clarke: "Ha, ha, ha, ha, ha."

73

"Here," Jenny said, handing me the chip that she had used. "We'll fly together."

"Nice arm," Clarke said to me. Then he pulled away on his bike. The sound receded. I was left alone with Jenny. I had made the right decision.

"Come on," she said, impatient. I thought she looked off-balance.

"Are you okay?"

"Come on," she said again.

I realized she wanted me to climb on top of her the way Clarke had. I did, and she started moving before I had a firm grip. I didn't fall off, though. I uploaded the chip she had handed me. When I looked over her shoulder, the world had changed. It was daytime, and I had to turn off my night vision. Instead of the cliff and the ocean we were in a dense jungle. The leaves hit against us as we drove along a narrow trail. Jenny's clothes had changed. She wore torn cloth that only just covered her enough to be decent. I looked down to see that I was dressed the same. "Whoa," I said, and held on tighter.

"Yeah," Jenny said.

There were sounds all around us. I realized they were animals. I was suddenly afraid. Up ahead, I saw a figure on an animal. It was Clarke. He was here too.

"Where are we going?" I said into Jenny's ear.

"Town."

We were gaining on Clarke. Jenny really could fly. Then we were in the town, although it wasn't what I had expected. The buildings were huts. Their construction seemed impossible; they were much too large, considering the wood and leaves that had been used to build them.

Clarke dismounted and the animals fell silent. "Whoo-eee!"

Clarke shouted, and he pointed his hands up in the air. "That should bring them running."

I realized that Clarke was seeing something else. I turned to Jenny. "Huts?" I said.

"Yeah, graybeard. Huts."

I reached a hand up to my face and felt that I did have a beard. I had been given a program. I was a robot. So why did this all seem so wrong?

A group of brutish-looking men approached. There was one girl with them, although she looked no older than a twelve-year-old human. I realized I wanted to hurt her. I looked at Jenny, but she wasn't paying attention to me anymore.

"Look at this group here," Clarke said.

"You started without us?" one of them said.

"Who's this humanoid?" another said, pointing to me.

I stepped forward ready to punch him in the face. I wanted to see what was inside him, and it seemed as good a way to find out as any. But Clarke stepped up and put a hand on my chest. "This no-good piece of shit is the man that's got your hookup," Clarke said. "Grog." He looked at me. "That's Grog, Cog, Smog, and Fairy." He didn't indicate which was which, and I didn't care to find out. "Check out my man's gun hand," Clarke said, holding up my right arm, which still sported a clamp at the end.

"Give with the sims," the one I decided to think of as Cog said.

"Ah-ah," Clarke said, spinning around to my other side. "Numbers first." And then Clarke cut through the group, everyone parting to let him by, and we all fell in line behind him. Jenny and the girl had their arms around each other. Cog fell into step with me.

"You're staying out at the beach house," Cog said to me.

"There's no beach here," I said. I looked around. There were small animals crawling on the tops of the buildings. "What are those?" I said.

Cog followed my gaze. "What do they look like?"

"Little people with tails and fur."

Cog shook his head. "Fucking hell . . . Clarke, you bastard, this one's already simmed up. Why the fuck do we have to wait?"

"Monkeys," Jenny yelled, answering my question. "Come here, boy," she called to one of them. I watched as he came to the edge of the roof, considered Jenny, and then ran off. "I guess he doesn't like me."

I moved up to join Jenny, more comfortable with her. I could tell that we were seeing the same thing.

Allistair's was a tiny one-room hut that was almost completely empty when we crashed in. Our little group seemed to fill the place immediately, and everything was suddenly too loud. It would bring the other animals from the woods. It would endanger us all. "Shhhhh," I said, but nobody heard me.

Allistair, or at least the person behind the counter, looked at us as though he had seen us all before, but he pulled a double take when he got to me. Clarke threw something down on the table, and then Allistair set chips out on the table for each of us. I took mine and uploaded. The numbers hit my system hard on top of the sim. I could feel my processes being kept busy trying to read the data, and as the numbers crunched everything got slower.

"Give 'em up," Grog said.

Clarke said, "Now, my boy."

I pulled the chips out of my pocket and they got passed around. Maybe the numbers were interfering with the sim, but the room no longer seemed to be the inside of a hut. It was now a square brick room, poorly lit. I saw that my companions all wore sweater vests and bowler hats, where before they had been dressed in the same tattered clothes I had. Some of them had removed simul-skin from various parts of their bodies. One of them had clamps for hands.

One of the patrons from the corner came up to us. He was an old robot, perhaps an order three, with no human features other than his form. "Hey, boys," he said. "Hey, boys." A chip got passed around to him. He took it back to his corner, bowing as he went.

I found another sim chip in my hand and I uploaded. The world didn't change this time, but everything seemed brighter. It was as if I could see what was going to happen before it actually happened. I could see that Jenny was mine for the night. What could I do? a part of me thought. I tried to message her only to find the numbers had frozen my messaging program.

"What are we going to do, Clarke?" somebody asked.

Clarke had Fairy in his lap. She was a full-size robot after all, I saw.

"Sapien was built by humans," Clarke said.

The group looked at me. I felt embarrassed and wished that Clarke hadn't shared the information. And then I was annoyed with myself, because usually I was proud of the fact that I had been built by humans. It granted me a sense of superiority that I was somehow closer to the creators, and I therefore had to be more like them. But here I knew that there was no value to that. Grog actually apologized to me, putting a placating hand on my back.

"More numbers!" Jenny yelled.

Clarke paid. We uploaded.

"Let's go," Clarke said. He moved like lightning. We all did, leaving sparks behind us. Outside it was night, and the town was as I had remembered it upon arriving several days before. But everything was rimmed with neon outlines. I tried to get next to Jenny again. She was deliberately staying away from me, I could see now. She had dangled herself in front of me back in the cabana, but for them it was all a game. *Bring out the human-built, he's so humanoid, it'll be great fun. What else is there to do in this town?* No, she was teasing me, and I had been stupid to allow myself to think anything else. I had come . . . Well, I couldn't think why I had come.

"Grog," Clarke said, and Grog came to his side. "Throw me." Clarke pointed at one of the windows nearby.

Grog picked Clarke up. The group stopped and formed a half circle around them. Grog pulled back and launched Clarke, who slammed into the window. The window broke, glass falling to the ground. The wood of the frame splintered, but Clarke didn't jump in, as I thought he might. He stood up, and the group waited. Nothing happened. Clarke stepped back. "Ha, ha, ha, ha, ha."

Smog went over to the window on the other side, reached up, and broke it with his fists. Clarke moved on and we all followed him. Jenny was beside me now. "Why'd we break those windows?" I said.

She shrugged. "They were there."

"What about those?" I said, pointing to one of the houses across the street, its windows still intact.

She shrugged again.

I knew I should say something about her hair . . . something so that she would pay attention to me. I didn't want to lose her attention.

Clarke stopped suddenly. "John Gropner," he said.

Fairy wheeled around with her arms out. "Wheeeeeee."

"Gropner," Smog said.

"No," Jenny said.

"For Sapien," Clarke said, looking at me.

"Clarke, you kill Gropner and you'll be sorry in the morning."

"You kill Gropner and you'll be sorry in the morning," Clarke played back Jenny's voice. "Look, last human, last human-made robot, it's only fitting." Clarke looked at me. "Well, not *last* human," he said.

When Clarke started moving again, everybody seemed to know where he was going. We passed through the center of town, where a large fountain was still running with water, the lights from inside causing the arcs of water to glow, or perhaps that was just part of the sim. Down the street from the fountain, there was a one-story house set back from the street; a small patch of grass formed a rectangle in front of the house. I was certain the grass was artificial. Clarke went up to the door as if he had done it many times, and knocked. I expected there to be no answer, as there had been in the house where he had broken the windows, but almost immediately the door opened. A small man stood in the doorway. It was immediately apparent that he was human. His body was bent, his face covered in whiskers—real, not like the gray beard that had briefly covered my face in the sim. His hair was white and wild. "Clarke," he said, when he saw who it was. He looked past him at the group of us standing on the sidewalk.

"Gropner, it's time," Clarke said.

"Is it?" the old man said.

And then Clarke reached forward, grabbed the old man, and held him above his head. As he turned and crossed the lawn, he extended his telescopic arms, raising the old man high into the air. The group of us was silent in the suddenly eerie quiet. Then Clarke threw the old man into the street. The sound of the old man's body hitting the ground was flat. If there had been any question before as to whether he was bio or robotic, the blood that flowed from his nose and right elbow made it clear. I thought I should leap forward and stop this. The blood was glowing red; it was clearly acidic, like battery fluid, dangerous, a good argument that would also protect this human.

Clarke descended on Gropner's form and kicked him in the face. Gropner made a sound.

Hadn't they known each other? Why would this man allow this? The rest of the group surrounded the man on the ground. Each took a turn kicking his body. Even Jenny rolled over his legs with her wheels. I closed in with the group, but I didn't participate. I opened and closed the clamp where my right hand should have been. The man's legs weren't in the right position anymore. They had been broken, allowed to flop at odd angles.

I looked around. A group of decent-looking robots stood a little way up the street, watching. I wanted to call to them, but I didn't remember how. I kept trying to send a message, but it only bounced in my system: "Help, help, help." I looked in the other direction and saw a family of robots standing on their front lawn watching as well.

Clarke and Cog seemed the only people interested in beating the man anymore, and then only halfheartedly. He wasn't dead; amazingly, he hadn't even lost consciousness but was moaning gently.

"Think there's anything good in there?" Cog said to nobody in particular.

Clarke looked up at the house. "Nah. Let's get some numbers." He walked away from the man on the ground, and we all followed him. Jenny had her arms draped over Fairy, and the two were singing, their high, feminine voices screeching in the night. I looked up at the sky. The stars seemed to sparkle with a greater intensity than was usual, almost flashing completely on and off, like a pulse, or perhaps a code. The sim must not have worn off yet. I had the sudden thought that the beating might have been part of the sim's environment, but when I looked back Gropner was still lying on the ground. The crowd of bystanders had grown. A young robot ran into the street, looking after us, and then, satisfied that we were really leaving, he took a running kick at Gropner's face. I didn't flinch; I didn't even experience the requisite surge of empathy that should have accompanied such a sight; I was numb to our gang's exploits, the sims and numbers coursing through my system deadening me. I was a dead thing.

Back in Allistair's nobody had moved. There were numbers already spread out on the counter, and everyone in the group took one and then fit themselves into a large circular booth against the wall. I passed up the numbers chip that was handed to me, and my rejection went unnoticed. Jenny was opposite me, still entangled in Fairy's limbs, laughing. They were sharing a sim and didn't seem to see anyone else at the table. We had just beaten a man to death! Well, he wasn't dead when we left him, but what human could sustain such a beating, especially one so old? There was no doubt that he was dying even now. Why?

"Why?" I said, turning to the robot next to me. Grog?

He didn't respond; he was talking to Clarke across the table. I tried my other side. "Why?"

This syllable—one letter, really—was so elusive, so important. It was this word that had sent me to Barren Cove, and perhaps this word that had sent me out that night. For all our perfections, our complexities, the intricacies of our systems, our ability to assimilate and synthesize information that was gathered through multiple sensory inputs—they built us ears! They built us eyes!—why had they given us this word, this question: Why? It was a hole in our design. It was what made us more like them. These other robots laughing around the table, deliberately conflating their systems, perhaps they didn't feel it, this hole inside them, because they were robot built. They had evolved, able to procreate, more bio than me, and yet less human. They still knew to hate. That had to be part of it.

"My dad's getting treads," Cog said.

"No he isn't," Grog said.

"He's getting fucking treads."

"My dad's lucky I don't just shut him off; he does nothing but sit in the house all day."

Hadn't I been promised a good time? I thought that I had. I tried to recall the data, but the numbers were still in the way. Why? I wanted to shout it—why!

Everyone at the table fell silent. The old man that we had passed a sim to before stopped just feet away from the table, no doubt on his way to beg another round, now frozen in fear at the silence.

Everyone looked at me. I had messaged them all. I stood up. There wasn't enough room between the bench and the table to stand, so as I stood, the table pressed up against the people across from me. "Why did you do it? What's the matter with all of you?"

Clarke smirked back at me. "How'd you lose your hand, old man?"

I pointed the clamp at him. "*You* lost my hand!"

"You're one robo motherfucker," Clarke said.

Cog picked up one of the numbers chips and tossed it at the old robot still standing a few feet from our table. I wasn't an old man, I wanted to say; *he* was an old man. He didn't even look human!

Clarke opened and closed his metal jaw and held out his hands. "What else is there to do?"

The girls were whispering to each other.

I turned to go out, but my legs caught on the bench and I fell back into the seat. Everyone else was waiting for me. I grabbed one of the numbers chips off the table and uploaded it. There was some light laughter at that. I leaned back. My systems were moving so slowly, so slowly. I knew that there would be a system error soon and I would have to shut down. I was happy for that; they could do with me what they wanted.

10.

"YOUR HAND ARRIVED," Kent said from across the table.

I turned and tried to remember being brought back to the cabana. The surf rushed in a smooth arc that foamed as it hit the shore. Seagulls provided the descant over the ocean waves. I sat forward, resting my arms on the tabletop; they felt so much lighter than they had the night before.

Kent held up a small cardboard box. "I brought it down so we wouldn't have a repeat of last time."

"Thank you," I said, watching him push the box across the table. "How long have you been sitting there?"

"Only half an hour. There is something pleasant about hearing the ocean waves, so mathematical and yet irregular. It's like watching the second hand on a clock and knowing that your internal clock will match it. Do you ever do that?"

I didn't answer him.

"You ought to try it. It can help the hours fly." He looked around as though he were seeing the place for the first time. "It is rather dismal, isn't it?"

"It suits my needs," I said. He didn't even begin to resemble the Kent recalled in Dean's files. Who was he?

He shrugged. "So you say. Do you need help with that?" Kent said, indicating the unopened box that sat on the table between us. He sat up, exposing quite a bit of one of his thighs as his bathrobe fell open.

I realized that he wanted to see the hand. Perhaps it was like his fascination with robot history. I leaned forward and grabbed the box. "I think I'll be fine," I said, opening it. The hand rested between two plastic pillows of enclosed air. It could be seen through the upper pillow, obscured by the plastic and the blue letters of warning that coated it. Apparently, the packaging could be deadly. I picked up the new hand with my good hand, holding it in front of my face.

"Ah," Kent said. "It is quite amazing, isn't it?"

It was disconcerting, and in that sense it *was* amazing. Was this a part of me? It would be. The coloring of my active hand matched the coloring of the inert hand it held, serving to emphasize their kinship. Despite our appearance of individuality, we were manufactured. I set the hand down.

"Well, you must be eager to get to it," Kent said.

"Yes," I said, although I wasn't. Something about Clarke's beliefs had shaken me—I had heard them before, of course, and seen the modified gangs of younger robots in the city—but seeing his anger the night before, his true rage, the conviction that all humans should be put in the ground for having kept us captive when *we* were superior to *them*, made me wonder if replacing the hand wasn't in some way selling out. We weren't limited to their corporeal form, so why emulate them? The thinking was logical, as out of control as Clarke seemed, but I couldn't muster the anger.

"I really am willing to help. I know quite a bit about these

things. It comes with the territory of collecting archaic machines. They are always breaking down."

Had that been an insult? I started to unscrew the clamp
from the end of my right arm. "I'm fine, really." Once the
clamp was removed, I set it down next to the hand on the
table. It didn't have the same emotional impact as the realistic
hand beside it. Here was a metal tool sitting on this table. It
had two prongs, screws at the hinges, and score marks at the
ends. It was like anything that had been discarded. But the
hand seemed significant to me. Which was what separated me
from Clarke and his friends, that belief in its significance. I
picked it up.

"You shouldn't feel unwelcome at the house," Kent said.
"Clarke is not around that much. And Mary and Beachstone
do keep to themselves."

"Thank you for the invitation." The part of the hand that
attached to the wrist had a metal joint protruding from it, and
there were wires to be connected.

"Yes, solitude. There is that too. How I know of that."

I focused on the task at hand.

"But it does get tiresome at times. There is the hope, sometimes, that there will be companionship."

"Is Beachstone never well enough to talk?" I said, attaching
a wire from my arm to the hand. I couldn't help but feel that
Beachstone had the answers I was looking for. I could understand all the other members of the family—even Clarke, it
seemed—and we all wanted the same thing, even if we had
gone about discovering it in such different ways. We wanted to
know why we should bother going on.

But Beachstone didn't have that luxury. He had to be able
to give me an answer.

"Oh, well enough is a matter of opinion, it seems," Kent

said. He readjusted his robe, although it hadn't shifted. He looked out at the water.

The hand, my hand, meshed with my system and I was able to move the fingers even though I hadn't yet joined the hand to my wrist.

"Quite amazing," Kent said, looking at my hand now.

I wondered if I had made a mistake, doing this in front of him. It seemed intimate and a bit shameful.

"I know that I have the knowledge inside me to build such a hand," Kent said. "I would have merely to access the files, assemble the parts, and I could construct a hand like that. And yet, this knowledge seems so foreign to me. It is almost as if it isn't there."

"That's why I ordered mine prefab."

"True. Very true."

I was having trouble connecting the hand to the wrist so that it clicked into place. My new fingers were flapping as I tried, as if they could somehow assist me.

"You know, I lived in the city once, for a little while," Kent said.

I looked up at him. "Really?" I had not gotten to that information in Dean's log.

"Focus on your hand," he said.

I looked back at it, the fingers now waving uncontrollably.

"Yes, for a little while," he said. His voice was mournful. "The city—that big machine. I think that the city was really man's greatest display of mechanical ingenuity, for isn't it nothing more than a robot of its own, a living thing with millions of mechanical parts that move to and fro, each contributing to the larger thing? Yes, the city for me was like losing myself in humanity. Everyone was interconnected. And I was connected to all of them. It is no surprise, then, that I fell quite in love when I was there.

"In the city there is almost an endless supply of junk shops, pawn shops, collectibles boutiques, small dusty places in which every imaginable surface is covered with the detritus of the past several centuries. There are glass-fronted counters and cabinets in which every shelf is filled with buttons, windup dolls, china, gas station glasses, souvenirs from defunct companies, low-order robots even. I tell you this because although you've lived in the city you may never have been to any of these places. In certain parts of the city, there are streets full of them, in which every single storefront is identical, the windows yellowed, bicycles in the front window with marionettes astride them. And in other parts of the city these stores are hidden, in basements beneath restaurants, or in walk-up apartments. These stores are almost always empty, which is why you most likely have never come across them. Very few robots are interested in the past, for so much of the past is the human past, and we, after all, are the future. So lonely proprietors—some human, some robot—sit in their dust-filled junk shops waiting for customers to come and look. And I went and looked. I looked at all of them. I was in and out of the stores all day every day. I would find treasures in these stores, robots that nobody would use the word *robot* for anymore. Unfortunately, none of the treasures I acquired in those days made it back to Barren Cove with me, but I have the collection I have.

"It was in one of these stores that I found my greatest treasure: a robot, not on display, but there for the same reasons I was. He was an order-six robot, human in appearance, and he was holding up a twelve-inch windup metal replica of the robot from the twentieth-century television show *Lost in Space*. He started to do the voice, 'Danger, Will Robinson,' but I finished it for him, and he turned, and he held up the toy as if to say, have you ever seen anything more glorious? And I hadn't. We shopped the rest of the day together. And the next day. And the day after that. His name was Michael. He shared my passion for pre-robotics-age robots . . . toys, I mean.

"It was not long before we were sharing a small two-bedroom apartment in an old building that had once been a hotel and had long ago lost its luster. Our combined collection, which continued to grow, made the apartment seem dark and not unlike the shops in which we spent our days. We discussed the relics that we dreamed of finding while sifting through the treasures before us. Some days Michael would go off on his own, claiming he needed time alone, and on those days I shopped by myself, finding that it no longer had the same kind of satisfaction it had with Michael beside me, but also knowing that if I didn't grant him some freedom, he would no doubt leave and never return. After all, hadn't I left Barren Cove for just that kind of freedom?

"But it became apparent that Michael's interest in our collection took a very different manifestation from my own. For I did then, and still do now, take appreciation in an earlier time's vision of myself, reveling in the particular idiosyncrasies of each individual toy. A toy that was meant to be a windup toy, for me was just a windup toy, but Michael, on the other hand, used the shells of these toys to 'create new life,' as he used to say. He wanted to turn them into higher-order robots, so that our apartment included many little robots with limited consciousness. These robots could do very little of value, except, I found, for one particular thing, and that was to wait on Jennifer when she began to come around to the apartment. Jennifer was Michael's owner. She was human, and it sickened me that he considered himself owned by her. It was so old-fashioned. It was disgusting. I have nothing against humans, and I relish their culture, but Michael was not something to be owned. Besides, he was mine.

"But from then on, I had to share him. In fact, I had been sharing him all along, for on the days that Michael had refused to join me he had spent them with Jennifer. Jennifer seemed indifferent to my presence, and in fact began to treat me as though I belonged to her as well. She delighted in Michael's little creations and was angry, as was Michael, that I refused to allow some of my more prized acquisitions to be altered in any way.

"There are many good memories that come from that time when the three of us would scour the various collectibles stores together, when Jennifer would bring to light some toy that we had missed and we would crowd around her, the three of us like the three wise men above the savior in her hand. But much of that time was agony for me, because I knew I no longer had Michael's attention all to myself and had discovered that I never had. I considered returning to Barren Cove, to make him jealous through missing me, but I was afraid that he would merely forget me, and that instead of the reunion I imagined on the beach, I would be alone with the few toys that I had managed to save from their Dr. Moreau machinations. So instead, I stumbled on the solution of bringing Barren Cove to me. I sent away for my sister. I can't say I was surprised when Beachstone arrived as well.

"And then we were five. And five, despite it occurring naturally as the number of fingers on each of our hands—excuse the reference—is an awkward number. Because, after all, isn't the thumb always somewhat excluded from the other members of the group? Yes, in the humans' minds, the thumb had a dominant position. Its separation was in fact what separated them from the rest of the animal kingdom; it granted them their superiority, and so they passed it down to us. The thumb is quite powerful. But it is also lonely. And so, I found myself the outsider in the little family of my own creation. Mary and

Michael, Beachstone and Jennifer, they were all thick with one another from the beginning. I had succeeded too well in bringing Barren Cove to me. I learned then that there was no running from your problems, because they were always with you and not easily shaken.

"We fell into a new routine. We added a nightlife to our days of shopping. There were still bars in those days that served both humans and robots, alcohol for the one and numbers for the other. These places were dark, and there were few questions asked. The waitresses brought what was ordered and didn't look at who consumed what. After all, I looked just as human as Beachstone, Mary just as human as Jennifer, Michael as human as all of us. There always seemed to be a great deal of trading places in those dark bars. I found myself at one time beside my sister, at another time beside Michael, and the others no doubt traded places as well. And yet, I couldn't help but feel as though my position at any given moment was an accident, because it was quite clear that Beachstone and Jennifer had an interest in each other that far surpassed any interest I could hope to elicit in either one, which would have been fine by me. I didn't care for Beachstone in those days, and I will admit that I don't care for him much now. And since Jennifer to me was an obstacle, the fact that they were willing to occupy each other suited me fine. Let their own kind stick together was what I thought. But much to my dismay, Mary and Michael seemed to have an interest in each other with almost the same degree of passion. And so, I was left with my numbers, which I could only hope would make me unaware of what was going on around me at any given time.

"I must have had quite a lot of numbers the night of the first incident, because I don't remember it with any clarity. We had stayed out until the bar closed, stumbling home at two in the morning. The city, despite its reputation, was quite asleep. The streets were relatively empty. The buildings were dark. We made it into the apartment. Some of the toys had been left on, and they greeted us at the door. I must have kicked one of the toys, because before I knew it Michael had pinned me against the wall. Jennifer was between us somehow, trying to pull Michael back, but he was furious. I had never seen him quite so passionate in any way, let alone angry, and even through the haze of the numbers, I was frightened. He showed no compunction over opening little metal toys and giving them enough awareness to realize they had meaningless existences—what would he feel about cutting open me, whom he had seemingly discarded for Mary? I wanted to strike back, and I tried to.

"I don't know if I was successful. Beachstone pulled Jennifer away. Mary must have done the same with Michael. My system overloaded, and when I rebooted it was morning. Michael and I gave each other quite a wide berth for the next few days, and I knew then that he would indeed kill me if he were given the chance. I was surprised to find that I might be willing to kill him in return.

"Everything was all right for a while, then. We returned to our normal condition. Michael and I even went shopping on our own, and one of my favorite memories from that brief respite is of a time Michael and I had reached opposite ends of a store and then turned to show each other a button that we had each found that showed a boxy robot taller than the buildings in the city, breathing fire, and knocking buildings down. We had found the same pin. We bought them both, and that is one thing I still have in my collection today. But despite our seemingly renewed love, Michael had managed yet again to have a secret life besides the one I was part of. It turned out I was to be an uncle.

"Beachstone and Jennifer might very well have had their own plans of a similar nature, for they grew secretive at this time as well. And while I thought that Michael and my relationship had been repaired, in fact, I was more than ever the odd man out.

"It was midafternoon on a Tuesday. The weather was impeccable, and even in the city the slivers of clear sky visible through the buildings made anything seem possible. It made it hard to imagine then, as it does now, that anything negative could possibly take place, not just at that moment, but ever. Dark and evil things should take place on dark and evil days. But I was not that fortunate. I had gone out on my own early in the day. When I returned home, I found that the good mood the weather had put me in was not unique. Beachstone, Jennifer, Mary, and Michael were celebrating. Their cause, it seemed, was a new robot whom I had never seen before. 'Come and join us,' Michael said. 'Meet your nephew, Clarke.' And with that he put his arm around Mary's waist. Well, you can imagine that this was the final straw for me. I had wanted nothing more than a world of my own, and yet again I had been forced out, my happiness stolen by my own family, my love rejected and abused. I attacked. It surprises me even now to say so, but I did.

"I rushed toward Michael first, but he was entwined with Mary, and so my attack ended up being on both of them. Beachstone was not going to let that stand, of course, and so by the time I had reached them, he was between us. I pushed him aside, cutting him, and attacked Michael, who was surprised by the assault and unprepared. I was able to turn off his systems before he could respond, and I proceeded to beat his inert body as everyone else tried to pull me off him. When you love somebody, you would rather they no longer exist than exist for someone else.

"The fight became confused. There were too many of us involved. In the end, Beachstone was badly injured; he's never fully recovered. Michael was dead, and Jennifer disappeared. I never saw her again. Mary brought us all back to Barren Cove and devoted herself to Beachstone. He was always sick now; he needed her constant care. It gave her something to do. Clarke and I were left to roam. I have my collection. He has his eccentricities. And Barren Cove protects us all from the memories by making them seem distant, making us numb."

I had managed to attach my hand as he spoke. The repair was flawless. I moved the fingers absentmindedly, reveling in the sound they made as they tapped against the tabletop. Kent had focused on a point out at sea, and he kept his gaze fixed on whatever was there that he saw. He seemed emptied by his confession. Gone were the normally flamboyant gestures, the amusement in his cheeks; even the affectation of his speech had disappeared to some degree. He was deflated by the emotion of the memories. Despite his claims that Barren Cove numbed him, he had needed to talk, and the pain was still raw.

"You fixed it," Kent said, indicating my hand.

I held up the hand and moved all my fingers. "I did."

"Do you feel whole again?"

I was taken aback by the question. Did I? "No," I said, shaking my head.

Kent stood up. "That's too bad," he said.

"Have you ever tried to find them?" I said, just before he stepped out onto the sand. "Michael and Jennifer?"

"My dear, I told you. Michael is dead. Spare parts won't make someone whole again. I try to reassemble my lost collection. That is something."

"Mary wants you, Master Kent," Dean said over the intercom.

"She is always in a panic these days," Kent said. "Beachstone is, after all, quite sick. That is why you are here." And with that he stepped out of the cabana and out of sight.

I considered for a moment trying to fit Kent's story in to what I knew already. "Dean?" I said.

"Yes, sir?"

"How long did Kent live in the city?"

"Ten years, sir."

I said nothing.

"Should I continue, sir?" Dean asked. I nodded, and she resumed her narration.

11.

KENT COULD SEE Kapec mowing the lawn that unnaturally covered the acres around Barren Cove, just as he had before Kent left for the city. The poor bastard, Kent thought, a constant struggle to tend, to keep alive, to make bow to his will these bioforms—the grass, the bushes, the flowers—so that they match a long-ago plan: living art, aesthetic living. He can never leave. And who comes out to see it? Yet there she is, the same Barren Cove I left, and I have Kapec to thank for that. Kent rode his yellow motorcycle up to the robot on the lawn mower. He shut off the engine; Kapec did the same; and the two robots sat astride engines, facing each other.

"You came back," Kapec said.

"Barren Cove is mine now."

"Master Beachstone has been sick."

"Master Beachstone?"

"You came back," Kapec said.

To have such simple thoughts must make life so much easier. To have such simple tasks. "Where is everybody?"

"In the back. Mary has cared for Master Beachstone through his sickness. She is always with Master Beachstone."

Perhaps it had been a mistake to go away. Kent had hoped that it was his father's weakness that made the human seem important, but if now that Father was gone Mary was serving him, and Kapec too, then Kent had indeed been away too long. He wouldn't wait to put that right. He started to dismount.

"Please don't leave that here, sir. I'm mowing the lawn."

Kent rolled the motorcycle alongside him and left it at the foot of the stairs to the porch. He messaged Dean as he mounted the stairs. "Where are Mary and Beachstone?"

"Welcome back, sir."

There was something grander about the house now that it was his. Barren Cove seemed to loom over him, so large, so Victorian, so different from the city. "Where are they?" he said out loud in the foyer.

"They are in the back. I'm sure Mary will be so happy to see you."

"I'm sure she will," Kent said. He continued through the house but stopped just inside the kitchen. "What did they do with Father?"

"They buried him, sir. Near Master Vandley."

What else did he expect? Father would have wanted it that way. He had decided to deactivate, after all. Kent crossed the kitchen and looked out the window onto the backyard. Two figures sat at the edge of the cliff, framed by the sky ahead of them. Mary, even from behind, looked unchanged. She wore a dress that he didn't recognize—yellow with a red paisley design—but otherwise, it was his sister. Beachstone, because the figure beside her could only be Beachstone, had changed considerably. He was taller than Mary now, but skinny, the shirt he wore tenting around his body, not even finding it when the wind blew. Kent was amazed, despite himself, and he had a moment of regret for having stayed away for so many years, missing a chance to watch this boy grow. This man grow. "I thought Beachstone had been sick," he said.

"He has," Dean said. "But today is one of his better days."

Kent almost messaged his sister, but then decided he would go to them in person. He went out through the back door and into the yard. It would be so easy to rush them and push Beachstone off the cliff. It would be over then. He had seen humans killed in worse ways. In the end, it didn't matter to the humans one way or another. Instead, he called when he was only halfway across the yard. "Mary."

She turned and her smile was instantaneous. She pulled herself up from the cliff edge and ran to Kent. She hugged him, something she had never done before, something he didn't think he had seen any robot ever do before. His arms remained at his sides, but he was surprised to find that he was relieved by the greeting. "You've missed Father," Mary said when she stepped back.

"I know. That's why I came back." He looked down at Beachstone.

"Kent," Beachstone said.

"Beachstone. You've changed."

"You haven't." Beachstone began to cough, little more than clearing his throat at first, but then the fit began to rack his body, and he heaved, folding at the waist. Mary dropped down behind him and put her arms around him, holding his chest and collarbone. "Breathe," she said. "Breathe." But Beachstone's breathing didn't sound much better than wheezing, a strain between coughs.

"Mary, leave him be," Kent said.

She looked back at him. "He's sick."

"So what do you hope to do by holding him like that?"

The coughing eased. Beachstone looked up at Kent through wet eyes, but he was still focused on evening his breath. "You've been gone a long time," Mary said.

Kent reached down and grabbed her arm. "That's right," he said, pulling her up. She gave at first, unprepared for the sudden violence, but then she braced herself. As always, they were evenly matched.

"Let go," Mary said.

"Come with me," Kent said.

Beachstone wiggled out from behind Mary. He had to push himself farther over the edge, his legs dangling, before he was able to climb back up to solid ground. The ocean churned below, its rush and crash endless. "You'll want to let go," Beachstone said, standing.

Kent saw that the human was taller than he now as well. The white scar that Kent had given him still stood out on his tanned leg. But he was skeletal; there could be no force there. Still, Kent let go of his sister. She went to Beachstone's side immediately, putting her arms around his waist. He put an arm around her shoulders as if he had been the one protecting her. Protecting her! I'm her brother, Kent thought. "What's been going on here?"

"Life," Beachstone said. "Just like everywhere else."

"I came back to run Barren Cove."

"Kapec and Dean do a pretty good job," Beachstone said. A gust of wind blew Mary's hair.

"I could kill you," Kent said.

Beachstone didn't say anything. Mary messaged, "Kent, please."

Kent looked at the two of them, his sister, and—what had his father said?—his *brother*, huddled together like lovers. He turned his back on them and went into the house.

Upstairs he searched through the rooms. His had been left untouched. Beachstone's and Mary's rooms looked lived in. His father's room, however, now appeared to be a workroom. The bed had been pushed into one of the corners, and a long wooden bench was set up along the far wall over which a pegboard hung lined with tools. Various wires, circuits, and spare parts littered the table. There was an old PC to one side, in addition to Dean's panel. Some of the materials Kent recognized from his father's old workroom, his own birthplace and the birthplace of his sister. He turned away from the room, as disgusted as he had been at his sister and Beachstone's displays of affection. Why had he come back? Because it was his right to. It was his home. It was his.

12.

MARY DIDN'T HAVE to go to Mr. Brown's just yet. Beachstone had taken ill again that week, spent most of his time asleep, and so the food supply was fine, but she was determined to continue her usual routine, if for no other reason than to show Kent what that routine was and that she valued it. And so, when Tuesday came, five days after Kent's return, Mary set out for town by foot as she always did, leaving Dean to watch over Beachstone.

The weather was beautiful, although the sky was a bit cloudy, and each time a cloud passed in front of the sun, Mary would look up, suddenly concerned that it was going to rain even though the barometer hadn't changed. Each time she found no sign of rain. She worried about leaving Kent and Beachstone alone. She remembered the way they had tortured each other growing up, and the time apart didn't seem to have changed their dispositions. But they would have to learn to live together. That was what Father had wanted. He had never forgiven Kent for leaving.

When Mary had left the house just now, Beachstone had been sequestered in his workroom, poring over the electronics texts that he had been studying for years. Kent needed to find a hobby as well. Maybe he could collect something. She would talk to him about it.

The wind blew off the ocean, carrying the sound of voices. Mary stepped to the edge of the path and looked down at the beach. Two naked human boys ran toward the water, and then as the waves came in, they screamed and ran away again. She watched them as they did the same thing once, then twice, then again. She scanned the beach for any sign of adult humans or robots. They must be children from town. She had never seen any children when she went to town, but there was nowhere else they could have come from. The sight gladdened her. She would go down to them. She turned, climbed over the cliff edge, and began scaling the cliff. The wind came in strong off the ocean, and she worried that she would tear her dress as she climbed.

The boys noticed her when she was still climbing, and they were standing not far from the base of the cliff when she came down. They both had their hands behind their backs. Mary found her eyes drawn to the little nubs of flesh sticking out from between their legs. "Hello," she said.

"Hi," one of them said. "You want to play with us?"

"My dress will get wet," she said.

"You'd have to take it off," the other boy said.

She wanted to very much just then. When was the last time she had jumped waves? She lived right at the ocean, they had the cabana on the beach, and yet, with Beachstone always sick, Mary hadn't actually been to the beach in . . . could it be years? She had time enough, she figured. "Okay," she said, peeling her dress over her head.

One of the boys giggled, and they both ran away as she dropped the dress onto the beach. She ran after them. Her hair blew out behind her. The first shock of water felt good. While the two boys ran away from the wave, Mary plunged into it, her nakedness soon hidden by the water. They seemed to like her again then.

"You're pretty," one of them said, standing in the shallows.

Mary was reminded of another human boy who had said something like that, and she was all at once ashamed that she had allowed herself to be deterred from her chore. "Thank you," she said. "Do you live in town?"

They both nodded.

"I'm going to town to get some food," she said.

"But you're a robot," one of them said.

"For a friend," she said.

The boys squatted. The water washed over the three of them, buoying up the boys while Mary's feet stayed on the ground. Another small wave came in, and one of the boys got some water in his mouth. He sputtered and then kept spitting, trying to free his mouth of the taste of salt.

"Do your parents let you get this far from town?" Mary said.

"We're here, aren't we?" one of the boys said.

"What are your names?"

"John," the one who thought she was pretty said.

"Martin," the other said.

The buzzing sound of an engine reached them from above the cliff. Mary zoomed in and could see Kent's yellow motorcycle skirting along the road up above. Her first instinct was to duck below the water's surface, to hide, but instead she stood up and started toward the beach.

"Where are you going?" John said.

"My friend's waiting for me," she said.

"We're your friends," Martin said, and the two boys followed her as she went back to her dress, which had blown closer to the cliff.

She turned to face them. John looked down. Martin giggled. "Yes, you are, but I've got to go," she said. She watched them both. "I had fun."

"Are you going to climb the cliff?"

Mary looked up. Kent had already passed where they stood. She hoped he hadn't gone after her. He'd get to town ahead of her and wonder why he hadn't passed her on the road. She could say that she had walked along the beach. "You can watch me," Mary said, pulling her dress onto her wet body. She turned to the wall and started climbing. She felt the boys' eyes on her, but when she got to the top of the cliff, she was surprised to find that they had already returned to the water, resuming their screaming match with the ocean, running with the waves. She was disappointed.

She turned toward the town. She zoomed to find Kent, but even at maximum magnification he was little more than a speck on the road. She hurried now. She tried to understand why she was so worried. He was her brother. They had had years together when they were inseparable, his silly experiments, exploring the grounds together, playing tricks on their father. But somehow he had changed. He had left because he was jealous of Beachstone. He had left angry. And he'd returned the same way. It hadn't been Father that he had been angry with, so why was he surprised that Father's disconnection hadn't proved a solution for him? She hardly recognized him anymore.

A robot couple laughed on the road ahead of her. She was near town now. She didn't recognize them, but then, she didn't know many people from town. Barren Cove was a world in itself. The couple held hands. As they approached Mary, they smiled at her pleasantly, friendly smiles different from the smiles they had been sharing, and didn't make eye contact.

Mary had the sudden feeling that she had changed too. She tried to understand what was different, running back through her memory, but it was merely made up of what she had learned and experienced, part of her, something she couldn't separate from her self: a caring, loyal daughter—the thousands of little tasks to support her father even up to his deactivation—a matron running a household in her brother's absence, a selfless caregiver, acts of love accruing—comprehending a hug, a kiss, a—Yes, she knew she must be different, because it was the only logical answer. Seeing her brother changed was like seeing herself. She had to reassess her data.

She turned to look at the couple behind her. As she watched, they ducked off the path and into the woods. In Barren Cove, she never lacked for privacy. There were Dean and Kapec, but they were just Dean and Kapec. Still, maybe Kent had been right to go away for a while. She wondered what the city was like. There were millions of robots there. She thought that could be frightening. Anyway, Beachstone needed her.

She entered town. She could tell that there was something unusual happening right away. There were more people on the street than usual, all laughing. Mr. Brown's store was in the same direction that the people were walking, and so she joined the crowd.

"Did you bring the present?" she heard a man say.

"I've got it right here, now relax."

"It's such a beautiful day."

"That's why they picked it."

Mary didn't know what the people were talking about. There was some kind of celebration going on, she knew. She was worried all of a sudden that Mr. Brown's would be closed, and that she wouldn't be able to get her groceries after all. But the crowd seemed composed solely of robots. There were fewer and fewer humans left, anyway. The boys, John and Martin, hadn't seemed concerned that they were missing any kind of festivity. No, Mr. Brown's would still be open. She could see the fountain at the center of town now. People were coming from other directions as well, and filing down Merchant Street.

"It's always exciting, isn't it?" a man said next to her.

Mary turned to see a stranger matching step with her, waiting for her response. "What is?" she said.

"A birth," he said. "The town celebrates like it has never happened before."

Mary could see a house down Merchant Street with balloons outside. Most of the crowd seemed to be milling around the front yard. Mr. Brown's, across the town center, had its door open. Mary looked for a chance to slip away; she didn't want to be pulled into anything.

"I didn't think I recognized you," the man said. "I can show you around if you want." His smile was so self-assured. "Such a pretty lady."

"No," Mary said, trying to cut her way through the crowd. "I've really got to go." She cut away from the man, ducking behind a family, and then she was out of the flow of traffic. Standing by the fountain, she could see that there weren't really that many people, that she had just been overwhelmed. She wasn't used to such crowds. She started across the square to Mr. Brown's.

"Ah, Mary," Mr. Brown said from behind the counter, looking up from the transistor television he had been watching. The store was empty, the lights off. "A lot of excitement out there today," Mr. Brown said, getting up and bringing a large brown paper bag up from under the counter. "Your usual."

"I didn't know," Mary said.

"The Internals. Their parents were RK-73s, but robots are taking their own surnames now. It's the young couple's first baby."

"Oh."

"How's Mr. Beachstone?"

"Today's a good day," Mary said.

"Good. Good," he said, his eyes already back on the television.

"'Bye, then," Mary said, backing out of the store.

"I'll see you next week." Mr. Brown had resumed his position in front of the television. There wasn't much business here. She wondered what she would do if he had to close his shop, or if he left to go to the city. It was supposed to be even harder for humans in the cities, she knew, but at least there were more of them. They could tend to their biological needs.

The square was mostly empty outside. Mary swung the grocery bag at her side, delighting in its weight—the same as every week—and the movement of her arm. It was a beautiful day, she thought. She looked in the direction of Merchant Street. Maybe she would go and see. She wasn't in any hurry. She started across the square and down the road. The crowd spread out in density from the house with the balloons, what must have been the Internals' house. As she approached, she saw that two folding tables had been set up on the edge of the lawn. One was filled with gifts and the other with numbers. It must have been expensive to have an open bar like that. Mary passed the tables, getting jostled on each side.

She felt uncomfortable at once. It had been a mistake to come. She didn't know these people. She didn't *want* to know these people. They were all talking. She caught stray group messages as well. She looked around suddenly afraid that the man who had talked to her in the square would find her and try to talk to her again. He had said she was pretty. Was she pretty? She realized only humans had told her that before.

People kept knocking against her bag. She was worried about the eggs. She brought the bag up to her chest and held it in her arms. Near the front stoop she saw three robots, two men and a woman, shaking people's hands. "Thank you, thank you so much," the man was saying. "It was time," the woman said to a group of women in front of her. They must be the Internals, she thought. Their son looked like a blend of the two of them. They were very good designers to have managed that. He was talking to a woman who must have been fairly drunk, because she put her hand out to balance herself several times, touching his shoulder, his chest, his arm. "I think my parents plan to show me around, but thank you," he was saying.

Mary found herself in awe. She was in awe of the couple and in awe of their child. All of these people around her had started like that, and all of them *could* start something like that. She knew inside her was the code, the mechanical skill, to do her part, to bring about another thinking thing, something that would be separate from her, and yet exist only because of her. The boy stood, talked, socialized, was very polite, functioned, and from what—pieces bought in the mail? A little time and energy? She understood why it was cause to celebrate. She wanted to celebrate on this couple's behalf—no, for herself. She was closed in by all these people. She started to make her way to the edge of the lawn. She needed to get out of the crowd. She needed to go back home and tell Beachstone. She needed to be on the beach again, in the waves. Maybe he would go with her. He was having a good day; she hadn't just been saying that to Mr. Brown. It had been too long since they had played in the water together.

She stepped out of the crowd onto the next-door neighbor's lawn. Immediately, a hand gripped her arm and started to push her. She almost messaged for help, but then she saw that it was Kent dragging her around the neighbor's house to their backyard. "Kent, stop it; let go."

"I want to talk with you alone," Kent said.

"Okay, just let go. You'll crush the groceries."

Kent let go. They were already in the next-door neighbor's backyard. The sound of the crowd was a hum, like the constant sound of the ocean at Barren Cove. "I came looking for you," Kent said.

"I saw you on the path."

"Why didn't you stop me?"

"I was on the beach." Mary stretched her arms out, reveling in the space. She was glad that Kent had found her. She could tell him some things about his behavior, and about the way things were now.

"Can you believe all this?" Kent said. "In the city, people have kids all the time—it doesn't mean anything, just one more person to catalog all this on a fresh hard drive." Kent looked at what was being stored on each of these robots' hard drives and then smirked. "And not this. What do robots care about nature?" He looked at the sky. "I don't care."

"You did once," Mary said.

He looked at her as if he had just remembered that she was there. "Don't tell me about what I did once. What happened to you? You're a slave now." He reached for the bag of groceries. "Look at this—getting food for that defective human."

Mary snatched the bag out of the way. "He's family. Father—"

"Father was a slave too, and I guess you're more like him than I am. Maybe that's why he liked you more than me, but

I'm not going to forget that I'm an Asimov 3000. I'm not going to forget that I own Barren Cove. I do. A robot."

"So what does it matter out here who owns what? Look around. What does it matter? A bunch of machines."

"You are a slave."

Mary turned away, but he grabbed the arm that carried the groceries, pulling on her. "You couldn't beat me when we were children," Mary messaged.

"You sleep with him!" Kent yelled out loud and messaged. "Don't even pretend, Mary. I've been home less than a week. You fawn over him, you sit with him like Father, you fetch for him, you sleep with him. What do you think's going to happen?" Kent came up to her. His face was ugly. He grabbed ahold of her again and pushed his body up against hers, vibrating, causing her to vibrate. "What do you think's going to happen? He's a human."

"And I love him."

"You're just a machine to him."

"No," Mary said.

Kent backed away. The sound of the party drifted into the silence. "I'll kill him."

"If you hurt him, I'll never forgive you."

Kent turned and disappeared around the corner of the house. The sound of his motorcycle seemed loud even from the backyard.

"Kent, no!" Mary messaged. She ran after him, but he was already gone. She knew she couldn't catch up to him, but she ran anyway. What would he do? He couldn't really kill Beachstone. He couldn't. She would never forgive him. She had said that. She ran. She crushed the groceries in her arms. She had to get there before Kent. She had to.

Barren Cove rose on the cliff ahead of her. She saw Kent's

bike parked out front, but she refused to believe that she was too late. He couldn't. She took the front stairs without pause and burst into the house. "Beachstone!" The house was silent. "Dean? Where's Beachstone? Beachstone!" Mary rushed upstairs. "Beachstone!" He couldn't have. Kent couldn't have. She rushed to Beachstone's room and stopped in the doorway.

Kent sat on the edge of Beachstone's empty bed.

"What have you done?"

Kent didn't answer.

Mary stepped toward him, dropping the groceries. The bag fell over, the broken eggs seeping onto the floor. "What have you done?"

"He no longer lives in this house."

Mary grabbed her brother. "Tell me."

"I didn't hurt him," he said, looking at her, his expression blank. "But he no longer lives in this house."

Mary stepped back, still staring at her brother. She did not recognize him. She turned and ran from the room.

13.

MARY MOVED BEACHSTONE'S workbench down to the
cabana piece by piece. Beachstone seemed to thrive living
closer to the ocean. The cabana had everything he needed—a
bathroom, a work space, shelter—and when Mary asked
about a bed, he said that he was fine sleeping in a chair. In
fact, Mary realized, Beachstone was barely sleeping at all. She
worried about that given his weak health, but all he wanted
was his tools, his computer, his parts. Kent allowed her to take
things out to him, a sort of silent approval. But Mary was to
spend the nights in the house. She accepted these terms in
order to keep Beachstone at Barren Cove. Father would have
wanted it that way. *She* wanted it that way. Beachstone seemed
unconcerned.

One day, Beachstone was sitting in a chair at the edge of
the open cabana door watching the ocean when Mary arrived.
The sky was unmarred by cloud or bird. A faint breeze blew,
just enough to offset the heat. "Hello," Beachstone said as Mary
stepped into the cabana with his lunch.

"Are you all right?" Mary said, concerned, so used to seeing him working.

He held his hand out to her. "More than all right." He waved her over. "Come." She came to him, and he pulled on her wrist. She realized that he wanted her to sit in his lap.

"I'll crush you," she said.

"No, you won't."

"I will," she said, sitting anyway, relearning what he had taught her so long ago without even knowing, to ignore what her logic told her in order to meet his needs. Or her own.

He took the sandwich from the plate in her hands and began to eat. "I feel good," Beachstone said. Neither of them mentioned Kent or Beachstone's exile. They looked at the ocean as Beachstone ate.

"Many people have never seen the ocean," Mary said.

"That's true."

"That's sad."

Beachstone ate. Then he raised his legs as best he could and pushed on her. "Okay, you're right—you're crushing me."

Mary got up. "I told you I was too heavy."

"You're right," Beachstone said, smiling.

"It's not funny. I liked sitting on you."

"What do you mean, 'you liked'?" Beachstone said, still smiling, but then the sound of a wave crashing filled the silence after the question, and his smile faltered. He looked at the water. "Let's go swimming," Beachstone said. He stood up and grabbed her hand again and started to pull.

"Wait," she said, reaching to put the plate down on the table.

"Come on," Beachstone said, still pulling.

Mary allowed herself to be dragged. "You just ate," she said.

"So?"

"You're not supposed to swim after you eat."

"No one ever told me that."

"It's common knowledge," Mary said.

"No one ever told me." They were in the water now, the waves fighting against their feet as they dragged themselves into the ocean.

Mary was able to access every time she had ever gone into the ocean—every time with Beachstone, and when she had gone into the water two weeks before with the two young boys. Now the sun was directly overhead. The surface of the water seemed to remain still, the water's motion coming from below. "What are we doing?" Mary said.

"Don't you remember?" Beachstone continued to pull them farther into the water. The waves now reached up to their chests.

Mary said, "I remember every time."

"So do I," Beachstone said, stopping and turning to her. "Look," he said, and he stepped closer to her, put his hands on her waist, and as the next wave passed, he lifted, raising her even higher. "I can lift you out here," he said.

When the wave had passed, both of their feet rested on the ground again.

"Your hair is wet," Beachstone said.

She grabbed his shoulders and pushed him under, letting go immediately, afraid as always to misjudge how long he could hold his breath, and especially now, so many years since they had gone swimming together and all the time he was sick. When he surfaced, she said, "So's yours."

He attacked her. She held him. "God, it's beautiful," he said.

They looked into each other's eyes. He pulled himself closer to her. She could feel that he was hard, excited. She knew what that meant, but she wished that she could understand what that meant. She hugged him, and he wrapped himself around her, and she remembered learning from him what a hug was, and then he kissed her. There had been glancing kisses before, brushes of his lips on her cheeks, but now he kissed her. She understood the affection, and she was glad for it, although it was nothing more than a conveyance of information for her. He loved her. He ground himself against her. She reached below and gripped his penis in her hand, knowing that was something she could do, and he pushed against her and gripped her, and he groaned, and she held tight as he moved in her hand, and then his penis began to go slack, and he looked in her eyes. "I love you," she said. His pupils were large, his muscles relaxed.

"I'm ready to begin," he said, after they had floated in silence for a moment, the waves drawing them farther from land.

"What?"

"Our son," he said. "I've studied enough. I'm ready to begin. I can build the hardware." He looked away. "And you can contribute software."

Mary thought of the party in town, the celebration that seemed to go on around her, without her. "I'll do what I can," Mary said.

Beachstone kissed her again. Then he tilted his head back, water running from his wet hair, and shouted.

Mary smiled back. When had she last seen him so carefree? And this was *with* Kent threatening murder and succeeding in banishment. She was happy, but as always, she felt as though she didn't quite understand.

"So why wasn't I supposed to swim?"

"You get cramps," Mary said.

Beachstone rolled his eyes in mock consideration. "Nope, I didn't get cramps."

"Well, your lips are turning blue."

"I'll race you back," he said, and he turned and began to swim.

The waves seemed to both assist and work against him. Mary outdistanced him quickly. When she turned back, she saw that he had stopped swimming. His face had gone pale, and his usual grave expression had returned to his face. Mary swam back to him. "Are you okay?"

"I'm fine," he said, out of breath.

Mary turned and latched his arms around her neck and swam them both to shore.

14.

I ROUNDED THE side of the cabana. The accordion doors were closed, and I stood in front of them wondering; I had left them open. After deciding that there was nothing to do but open the doors, I pulled them back expecting to find Clarke there. Instead, I found Jenny leaning against my chair.

She looked coy. "I hadn't seen you since that night," she said. "I was kinda worried."

I looked behind her, wary. She had been so disinterested that night. "Where's Clarke?"

"Why should I know?" she said, angry at the question.

I wanted to say something to make her even angrier. After all, what right did she have to visit me? We were no one to each other. She had been worried about me? She had made it abundantly clear last time that at best, I was worthy of being ignored. I thought about the way she had hung on Fairy all night. But then I wanted to make nice. It was ridiculous to cut myself off because I was jealous; she was here now. "I'm sorry," I said, sitting down beside her.

"Okay," she said.

"Okay," I said. Her body was close. Aside from the wheels and the hair, she had not gone into any of the body modification of her companions. Her simul-skin was unmarred and clean. I wanted to touch her.

She touched me first, putting her hand on my arm and leaning toward me. "You're so interesting," she said.

"No," I said.

"You're really human built?"

I nodded.

Her hand was rubbing my arm. She drew her hand down to my new hand. "You replaced your hand."

"Yes."

"Why are you living out here?"

"I needed to get away from the city. I had to do some thinking."

"And have you done some thinking?"

I looked at her, thinking just then, thinking that she was leading me on, and yet leading me on to what? She had come here and was showing interest.

I was such an old robot.

Fairy's arms around Jenny flashed in my mind. "I don't know," I said. "I think I have, only I'm more confused."

Jenny rolled off then, taking her hand away. The abandonment hit me hard. I needed her back.

"Why'd you change your legs?" I said.

"Aren't I beautiful this way?" she asked, spinning for me, her hands held palms up at her shoulders.

"Yes," I said.

"Then what's your question?"

I didn't know.

"Besides," she said, examining the walls of the cabana, "it's what people are doing." She shrugged. "Is it true that in the city people are deactivating? Especially fourth-order robots?"

"Yes," I said. That had been all that had filled the news when I left—another reason to get away.

She looked out at the ocean. "I'm faster than anybody in town," she said.

I wanted her to come sit with me again. I wished that I had sims or at least numbers to offer her, to share with her. There was Mary's way, and there was Kent's way, and there was this way, and right now, I wanted this way. I wanted to get lost in Jenny's pink hair and maybe even to build a robot. I had never had a child, and given the state of my mind, inert and nihilistic as it was, having one would seem to be hypocritical, but wasn't my desire for Jenny so, too? Wasn't my continued habitation at Barren Cove? "Come sit with me," I said.

"No," Jenny said, wheeling in front of me. "I just wanted to make sure you were all right."

"Please come back and sit with me. I'm very unhappy and you're all that's making me happy right now."

"No. I can't."

"Why not?"

She didn't have an answer, so she sat next to me, but she kept her hands in her lap and her eyes on her hands. Where had such prudence come from? I found my earlier courage, and I traced the outline of her arm with my new hand. "You are so beautiful. Ever since I saw you that first day I have wondered if maybe you were why I was supposed to come here."

"Like fate?" she said, with a smirk.

"Maybe so."

"Even the humans didn't believe in fate when they died."

I wanted to scream, *They're not all dead.* We saw one to-gether. But I wanted her to like me. Maybe if she liked me, I could like me too. I brought my hand up to her pink hair, and she pulled away, standing again. "Please," I said, not entirely sure what I was begging for.

"If you still feel that way, come meet me at the clearing in two days at noon," she said, and then she was gone.

I ran out onto the beach, but as she had said, she was the fastest robot in town. She was far gone, and running after her was fruitless. But she had said that she would meet me at the clearing. Where was she going now? To Clarke? To Fairy? Why did I care?

I turned back to the cabana. What was I going to do now? What was I going to do tomorrow?

I watched the water, not even wanting to go for a swim.

15.

THE FORM LYING across the countertop was humanoid. The metal skeleton was arranged in the proper configuration—the spine ran down the center, with a perpendicular crosspiece at one end, and another crosspiece set six inches from the other end. On each of these crosspieces there was a ball joint, the same technology that had once been used to replace bones in humans, and in each ball joint were more metal bars, forming, what was recognizable only because of the position, arms and legs. The skull still remained set aside. The lower part of one of the legs had been partially covered with padding and simul-skin, only the simul-skin had not been applied correctly, and it sagged, misshapen, stretching, grotesque.

Kent had been appalled when he found the half-formed robot. He shouldn't have been surprised. What did he think Beachstone was doing with all those tools? What sickened him was the part that his sister must have played in his experiments. It was little consolation that Beachstone seemed inept at robotics.

Kent heard his sister go into her room. At least she knew who was boss. He kept her in the house at night so that she wouldn't sleep down there with Beachstone. He strained for sounds of her, but she was silent. She must have already shut off for the night. "Dean, is my sister awake?"

"No, sir."

She couldn't bear being awake in the house. He should sleep as well.

"Do you want me to inform you when she awakes, sir?"

"No," he said, standing up. He walked over to his dresser. There was a toy motor that he had played with as a child sitting on top of it, coated in dust. He hadn't done anything mechanical in so long. The city had just been sims and sims. He wasn't sure he had ever seen anything outside of his one-room apartment. Who did Beachstone think he was, trying to build a robot? A human! Kent grabbed the small motor, dismantled it, and rebuilt it in less than a minute. The dust settled back onto the dresser top. The lights in the room cast odd forms on the walls and the floor. He turned on his night vision but the forms stayed, white now.

"What do they do down there?" Kent said. "Is she helping him?"

"I cannot say, sir."

"You can't?"

"I do not know, sir."

Dean's voice. It was Barren Cove. It was home. It made him sick. He couldn't imagine being anywhere else. He turned and looked at his room. It seemed empty despite the furniture. What was there to do?

He remembered the half-formed robot in the cabana.

He crossed the room and went into the hallway. His sister's door was open. She wanted him to know that she had nothing

BARREN COVE

to hide. But she had everything to hide. He stood in her open doorway, looking at her as she slept. He could deactivate her right now. All she had was her emergency safeguard to protect her. The sight of her so vulnerable angered him. He almost never rebooted. It was demeaning. He stepped into her room. She kept everything so precise, it was impossible to know that anyone lived here. The way the empty perfume bottles and silver candlesticks were arranged on her bureau was probably the way that Mr. Vandley's daughter had left them before either Mary or Kent was born. So obedient. He crossed to her, standing in front of her chair. Whose face had she been modeled on? Had their father even had a face in mind? Kent felt nothing about it; it was just his sister.

What would the robot in the cabana look like? Who would it be?

Kent jumped onto his sister's lap, facing her, his legs on either side of her own. He rearranged her hands so they were sitting on his thighs.

"You know what they do with robophiles in the city?" Kent said to her sleeping form. "The humans kill them." Kent grinned. "The humans kill them and they deactivate the robots and we let them."

Mary remained asleep.

Kent watched her. Why didn't she understand that the humans undermined their way of life? It was only a matter of time before all the humans were dead, and only robots were left, the superior being, continuing the clockwork of life. That's what she didn't see. Robots were alive. He was alive. And he couldn't die. Beachstone was an inferior being.

Kent wished he could reactivate her. He wanted to tell her now, so that she would understand. But there was no way. He had to wait until the time that she had set her system to boot

127

up. He watched her, wondering how his father had gotten her hair. Real human hair. It was all synthetic hair now—synthetic everything.

The sun began to rise, a faint light showing behind the curtains. Kent grew excited. It was hard to believe so much time had passed. He knew Mary's face by heart.

A faint buzz came from the back of Mary's head, and then she began to move. Kent grabbed her by the throat. "Good morning."

Normally they would have been evenly matched, but her systems were still booting up. She pulled at his hand. "Let go of me," Mary messaged him.

He reached up with his other hand and inserted the USB plug in his fingers into her USB port. She struggled, but he held her down. "Humans don't build robots anymore."

"No," she messaged him. Her face contorted. "No."

"You think you can make something with Beachstone?" Kent said.

"No."

He pulled his finger back. The program was activated. They would build their own robot. Kent could do it now with or without her, but she would be a part of it, she knew. It was part of her system now. He let go of her and stood up. "They kill robophiles in the city."

She stayed in her chair, not moving.

He was angry with her for being still. Was she so submissive? "I'll be upstairs," he said, and walked out. He listened for a sound behind him but heard nothing.

16.

CLARKE, ONLY THREE days old, was allowed to roam on his own for the first time. His parents, especially his father, had spent most of the past two days making sure that all of his systems were operational. They had kept him around the house, making him attempt simple tasks as he followed them around—sit, walk, talk. Almost immediately, Clarke had bristled under the attention. He was fine. He could feel that he was fine. All of his activity was conducive with the knowledge already installed on his hard drive. He started to tell them he was fine. His father was angry at first: "You'll listen to me." But his mother was nervous, taken aback, as if every word he said was a physical assault. And so, at last, with a sense that they wanted to be rid of him, Clarke was allowed to wander.

He went down to the beach. The sand shifted beneath his feet. He knew about the ocean, the tides, the sand, what they were made of and the theories as to how they were formed, but the feel of the sand shifting beneath his feet was wholly new. Of course, it made sense. The granules would move if acted upon, but the sensation of the ground giving way before him, holding him back from each step, was something to be registered, added to his memory. He walked to where the sand was pounded flat by the waves, but not so far that the water reached his feet as it rushed in and then rushed out, topped with foam. Would the water carry sensations that he couldn't know without experiencing them? He wanted to rush forward, but something held him back. Going in didn't seem like a good idea.

"You must be Clarke," a voice said behind him, and he turned to find a skinny man with long hair leaning on a driftwood cane.

"Beachstone," Clarke said.

"That's right. Well, he was able to do it. You appear flawless."

Clarke didn't know how to respond. He found that he had an intrinsic apprehension about this man. He must be dangerous. And yet, Mary had said, You must meet Beachstone; as soon as your father isn't around I'll take you to meet Beachstone.

"Well, welcome to the family," Beachstone said, holding out his hand.

Clarke took it; they shook and then let go. "Thank you," he said. This man was human, wasn't he? How could he be part of the family? Maybe he thought he was a robot.

"Just watch out for your father," Beachstone said. "I'd watch out for everybody."

"Including you?"

"We'll just have to see," Beachstone said, and turned away. He started to walk toward the small building nestled along the base of the cliff.

Clarke watched the man walk. He rested quite a bit of his weight on the driftwood cane, limping as he went. Clarke was confused by the encounter. If that was a human, how could you tell the difference? He looked just like Clarke did. Not the exact same features, but the same kind of features. They were indistinguishable. And yet, he had already heard his father say many times how superior robots were. Was it because Beachstone needed a cane? Beachstone disappeared into the cabana, and Clarke turned back to the ocean. He would ask somebody about Beachstone. For now, he wanted to explore.

He thought again about going into the water but couldn't bring himself to do it. Instead, he started down the beach, walking just above the limit of the waves.

The sun is almost perpendicular with the ground, Clarke thought. It is almost noon. The waves come in on average once every twelve seconds. The world is a constant flow of data, calculable, checkable, and much as expected. Already, Clarke looked forward to something new and different.

Two small figures played in the waves ahead of him. Clarke zoomed in and saw that the figures were small. In fact, in his limited experience, they were the smallest robots he had ever seen, and he wondered why anyone would build diminutive robots. But when he came closer and the two figures stopped to stare at him, he realized his mistake at once. These were humans, children. This, Clarke thought, is what makes us different. I'm younger than they are, but I am fully grown. What a waste of energy for them.

"Hey," one of the boys said.

"Hello," Clarke said.

"Can you climb?" the other boy said.

"Climb?"

"Yeah, this lady came by once and she could climb the cliff all the way up." The boy pointed to the cliff, but Clarke didn't turn. He knew what the cliff looked like. Instead, he watched how the children needed to look at the cliff as if to reaffirm that it was still there.

"I can climb," Clarke said.

"Do it."

Clarke was both compelled and repulsed by the command. He wanted to climb, and yet, if he climbed now after having been told to climb, somehow the climbing would be tainted, not belonging to him, but to this boy.

"Come on," the other boy said, and the two of them ran up the beach, sand spraying out behind each footstep. When the boys reached the bottom of the cliff, they started to climb. The light-haired boy raised a foot, leaning back almost parallel with the ground, trying to reach the top of a rock that was too tall for him. He steadied himself against the rock wall. The other boy had both hands over his head, his fingers splayed on the rock face. He looked back at Clarke and then up at his goal. Clarke joined them. He grabbed the wall and began to climb at once, the metal fingers beneath his simul-skin gripping the rock hard enough that little rivulets of dust dropped down onto the boys below him.

"Hey, wait for us," they yelled, but Clarke didn't want to wait. He wanted to show them that he could do something they couldn't do. In fact, he could do lots of things they couldn't do. They were useless. "No fair," one of the voices reached up the rock wall.

Clarke looked down. Both boys had stopped trying to climb and were watching Clarke's progress. I'll show them what they're missing. They'll see. Clarke started back down. When he hung just above the ground, he turned and looked over his shoulder. "Come on," he said, now in control.

The boys rushed forward, each gripping one of Clarke's shoulders and sliding off.

"No, you, what's your name?"

"John," the dark-haired boy said.

"Come around here." Clarke grabbed John and fit him in front, with the boy's back to the rock wall and his arms wrapped around Clarke's neck. "Now, you get on my back."

"Martin."

"Martin, get on my back." The blond boy climbed onto Clarke's back, and Clarke started climbing again. John strained to see past Clarke's head, to look below. He gripped tighter and then looked up into Clarke's face and smiled. They were halfway up the cliff now.

"Mary didn't let us do anything like this," Martin said behind Clarke's back. He readjusted his grip.

"Mary?" Clarke said, stopping at the name.

"The woman who climbed for us before."

"And got naked," John said, and the two boys laughed.

"That's my mother," Clarke said, angry that the boys were laughing.

John tried to stop laughing, looked down, and grew sober at the sight. "Whoa."

Martin grabbed John's left wrist in his right hand and kicked out with his legs.

"Hey, stop kicking," John said, shifting his position.

"I'm slipping."

Clarke started to climb faster. Martin readjusted his grip again.

"Quit it," John said, and kicked back.

Martin grabbed at Clarke and said, "Stop it."

Clarke hurried, taking less care to find handholds. What did it matter anyway? With his hands everything was a handhold. He could climb a cliff face with two humans holding on to him when they couldn't even climb it themselves. He moved faster not to reach the top before Martin lost his grip, but precisely because Martin might lose his grip if he moved faster. He wanted to see what would happen if the boy tumbled down to the rocks below. Clarke knew he could jump from this height unharmed—his systems knew it instinctively. But he had a feeling the outcome would be different for the humans. His preprogrammed memory units told him that. But could he trust his parents' programming? Had Mary mentioned two boys on the beach?

Martin's hands slipped away, and he gripped more tightly with his legs. He swung himself back up, gripping one of Clarke's shoulders, pulling, slipping, catching again. John reached for him, and in so doing, he shifted his own legs, which released Martin's grip, and suddenly the weight on Clarke's back was gone.

"Martin!" John yelled, letting go and trying to reach down to catch his friend, but the cage created by Clarke's body prevented him from getting anywhere. "Go down," he said.

They were at the top of the cliff, however, and Clarke brought them up on the ledge. John stood at the edge trying to look down, but the cliff jutted out, blocking his view. He looked back at Clarke with wet eyes. Tears drew lines in his sand-dirtied face. "You killed him," he said.

The boy had fallen. Clarke wanted to go back and see what had happened. He understood that John's reaction was telling him something, that the tears bespoke sadness, but Clarke didn't feel anything himself, just slight curiosity.

"We have to go back," John said. "Maybe he's okay."

Clarke knew that there was no way that the boy was okay. The knowledge he had been programmed with pertaining to humans told him this, and yet, this human, who must surely know his own kind better than Clarke could, had doubts as to the outcome of his friend's fall. How was that possible? Clarke picked up the boy without a word. With John in his hand, he felt a sudden urge to throw the boy off the cliff after his friend. It would be so easy. It would be so much fun. Yes, that was what this day was all about—fun. The world was a series of data points, but as time passed, there had to be a better way to occupy his operating system than counting the grains of sand, or mapping the fractals of the ocean waves. That's what these humans had understood. That was what John's face had said as Clarke had climbed. And yet, the climbing hadn't been the fun part for Clarke, whereas it had been for the boys. It was the boys' reaction. As he was reacting now, kicking and screaming and crying. Then Clarke pulled John's jerking body to him, and jumped off the cliff. John screamed the whole way down, and then his breath was knocked from him when they hit the beach. Clarke dropped him, and John coughed, dry, heaving coughs, as he crawled on hands and knees on the sand.

Clarke looked and saw what they had come to see. Martin's head had missed a jagged rock by only inches. Instead, the rock had caught the boy's shoulder; his right arm was almost broken off from his body, white bone gaping out of the torn socket, brown blood black with sand. His legs were at impossible angles, but his face was almost serene.

John had crawled toward his friend, had another bout of coughing, and then turned away. "I want to go home," he said.

"Are you happy to be alive?" Clarke said, turning to look at John, whose face was hidden in his forearm.

The boy cried.

"I can kill you at any time."

"Just take me home, please."

"I can kill you at any time."

John said nothing, not even looking at Clarke.

"No," Clarke said, answering the boy's request. "I took you to the top of the cliff and back. You go home yourself."

The boy made a sound. Was he still crying? He started to walk away. He dragged his feet in the sand.

Clarke looked back at what had once been a human. He looked at his own hand. He opened and closed his fingers and then ran his fingers one by one. He was indestructible. A wave crashed behind him. He turned and ran toward the water, not stopping when his feet felt the water pulling the sand out from under him, but plunging forward into the undertow. He dropped forward, the water splashing under his weight. A wave crashed over him, and the water pulled his body away from the shore. The world beneath the water was in constant motion. Clarke saw particles of the ocean floor being churned up by the waves, the brown wisps of smoke twirling and playing. For what? For Clarke to see at just that moment, to record on his memory chip forever. He rolled over, the sky coming into view. The sun was at a 110-degree angle to the ground. Clarke was far from the shore. He moved each of his fingers one by one, starting with the pinky on his left hand and cycling to the pinky on his right and then back again. He looked down the shore in the direction that John had walked. He zoomed in and saw the small figure making his way down the beach. He was bringing his feet up higher now, small tufts of sand like wings at the back of his heels. Clarke could kill that boy. He could end his life. He had ended Martin's life. Well, it hadn't been him per se but in fact the human's own inadequacy. His own small hand's inability to serve its purpose, to keep the greater form alive. His hands had slipped. And yet, John had accused Clarke of killing his friend. Clarke liked the accusation. Martin wouldn't have been in the position to have his fall if it hadn't been for Clarke. Yes, he had killed the boy. So fragile, the bioforms. So useless.

Clarke was beyond the waves now. Why had he hesitated to go into the water before? He was waterproof. He was indestructible! His mother had climbed for those boys. The thought stopped him. Before he had been built his mother had climbed with those boys. One of those boys was now dead. They had liked his mother. They had laughed at seeing her naked. Clarke ripped his own wet clothes from his body. He was a robot. All of this simul-skin that made them laugh, that made them think of themselves, what did it really have to do with them? Clarke knew of sex. Clarke knew of prudery. But his mother was a robot, as was he, and he had killed one of the humans and he could kill the other one at any time. He began to swim toward the shore. His hands cut through the water as his arms brought them around and around, the metal joints at his shoulders turning smoothly. He propelled himself forward. A wave swelled, trying to pull him away, but he climbed it and it then pushed him toward the shore.

When he stepped out of the water onto solid land, he was naked. He had drifted away from Martin's body. When he zoomed in, John was still visible on the horizon. Clarke wasn't interested in either of them now. He wanted to tell his mother about his day. He wanted to remind her of the boys she had seen before he had been activated. He wanted her to know what he had done. He knew how she would react. He knew how his father would react as well; he'd be thrilled. And yet, it was his mother's reaction that he looked forward to. John had cried, or at least there had been tears in his eyes. What would a robot's face do?

He started toward Barren Cove. The sun dipped over the edge of the cliff, casting the beach in shadow. The temperature dropped four degrees. He would have to pass Beachstone's hut again to get to the house. Watch out for everybody, the human had said. Everyone should watch out for me, Clarke thought. Clarke wondered what Beachstone's reaction would be to know that he was now living with a homicidal robot.

The weather seemed to change suddenly. Clouds that had seemed benign before, gentle white tufts drifting in the sky as the earth turned, now covered all of the sky in front of him. They were dark in the center.

I don't have to pass Beachstone's hut, Clarke thought suddenly. I can climb the cliff face. Of course I can climb the cliff face.

There was a change in the barometric pressure, and the air was suddenly soupy. Clarke climbed the cliff, rushing up to the top this time, unburdened by any weight, uninterested in the act of climbing, merely focused on getting from one place to the other. At the top of the cliff he flexed each of his fingers in turn once more.

Barren Cove was visible ahead. The sky that served as its backdrop was black. Clarke zoomed in. Was it raining there already? It looked like it was. He looked up at the sky overhead. A fine mist hit his naked form, like sea spray, but the sea was now far below. Along with Martin's body.

I am a robot. Built by two other robots. The rain began to fall, and then it was torrential. Clarke walked through the sudden nighttime as if nothing had changed. He was nearly at Barren Cove now.

The yard was empty. Kapec must have known enough to get out of the storm. Dean welcomed Clarke as the front door opened.

"Where's Mom?"

"Upstairs," Dean said. "In her room."

Clarke took the stairs two at a time. Lightning crackled outside. He went to his mother's door.

She stood at the window with her back to the door. The world outside was black, the pane of glass acting as a mirror, reflecting his mother's face back to him. Her face was strained, her eyes searching for something that she couldn't see. She turned to him suddenly. There was no change in her expression, not even at his naked form.

Clarke stepped into the room. A puddle of water had formed where he had been standing.

Mary looked away again, staring back out the window.

Clarke wanted to tell her that he had killed a human. That he had liked it and wanted to kill more. Her reaction would be terrible. He just had to say it. But he couldn't bring himself to form the words. "Aren't you even going to ask me where my clothes are?"

"Where are your clothes?"

"I took them off to go swimming."

A hint of a smile showed at her lips. Or was it a trick of the reflection? "That's nice."

If he said it, she would turn; she would pay attention. How was it that the weakened man on the beach held all her attention, that she managed to seem sick without him? The lightning flashed. "Mom," Clarke said.

Mary didn't turn.

Clarke crossed the room, knocked over some things on his mother's bureau, and then sat down. He listened to the rain while his mother stood looking at what? Her own image in the window? The ocean? The two of them were silent.

• • •

The storm lasted on and off for four days. Clarke stayed near his mother when she was in the house, bristling with his secret homicide. When Mary went down to the beach to be with

Beachstone, Clarke sat with his father and listened to the older robot rail against Beachstone while he dismantled and reassembled a small engine. On the first day that dawned sunny, Clarke left the house before his mother did. He found himself retracing his steps of several days before, stopping at the place where Martin's body had rested. Somebody had retrieved the body, and any sign of blood had long ago been washed away in the rain, but Clarke swam again, enjoying the feeling of the water on his simul-skin. It wasn't long afterward that he decided to return home. He would tell his mother about killing Martin. Maybe he would even threaten Beachstone for the entertainment value. It would certainly make his father proud.

He entered Barren Cove and started upstairs. He stopped at the sound of his mother's voice.

"Attach green to green and blue to blue."

"I know," a voice answered.

Who was Mary talking to? His father had made it clear that Beachstone was not to be in the house. "Not Kapec?" Clarke said, smirking, the joke automatic.

A racking cough came from down the hall. It was similar to John's heaving cough over his friend's dead body. It came from the stairway. Clarke walked quickly to the end of the stairs, looking into each of the open doors of the hall as he passed. Clarke climbed the steps to the upper floor. He knew that this was where he had been built, where, in fact, his parents had been built by his grandfather, and yet he had not been up the stairs since first being activated and had almost no data pertaining to the space. But when he came to the top of the stairs, he did not take in his surroundings but instead focused on the people in the center of the room.

Beachstone, his cane leaning against the edge of the table before him, bent over Kent's prostrate body. Mary stood at the end of the table near her brother's feet. Much of Kent's simul-skin was peeled away, revealing the metal skeleton beneath. Beachstone looked up. "Ah, you're early."

"What are you doing?" Clarke said.

"Making some necessary adjustments," Beachstone said, bending back over his work. He took several cables, attached them to ports in Kent's open chest, and then ran the cables back to a laptop sitting on a bench nearby.

Clarke tried to register the sight before him and access the appropriate response, but his systems seemed stuck in a loop. He looked to his mother.

"Beachstone is only doing what is best," Mary said.

Beachstone was sitting before the laptop now, typing.

Clarke understood what was happening—his father was being reprogrammed—but he didn't understand how or why. The sight of the featureless metal skeleton encased in the open crust of simul-skin was surprisingly startling. Clarke saw Martin's broken body on the beach. Beachstone was here doing the same thing. No, Beachstone was doing more, because all that Clarke had been able to do was to destroy. But here, Beachstone was changing Kent's life. He was erasing the Kent of the past and creating a new Kent that would reside in Kent's shell. Clarke knew that his parents had been robot built—that he had been robot built—but despite that legacy, here was the all too clear evidence that the humans built robots first. Clarke didn't like the idea that this frail human, whose own systems were so faulty that he needed to walk with a cane, was in some way superior to him. He could step forward and end his life with one blow. "You're killing him," Clarke said.

"I'm giving him a new life," Beachstone said.

"What was wrong with his old life?"

"If I told you the truth, you would never forgive me."

"You are in the process of killing my father. How do you think I will ever forgive you?"

Beachstone turned from the computer and looked at Clarke over his shoulder. "Your father raped his sister, and now we have you," Beachstone said. He turned back to his work.

Clarke looked at his mother again, but she was engrossed in the details of her brother's open body. Clarke didn't have to ask if it was true. He could feel it just by being in the room. And yet, instead of hatred, he felt respect. Beachstone had warned him not to trust anybody. And here Beachstone was proving that point. Yes, Clarke was superior to the humans, more powerful, indestructible, but this human . . .

You don't fuck with Beachstone. He will fuck with you all the way back.

I could kill him, he thought. But then, why hadn't he told his mother about killing the boy?

Beachstone continued to type as Mary watched him with awe.

I will not be fucked with either, Clarke thought.

17.

IT WAS SOMEHOW in the low fifties, gray and rainy, when the temperature had been in the seventies only two days before. Despite the weather, Mary found Beachstone sweating in his shirtsleeves with the cabana doors wide open, stooped over a tablet that was resting on the edge of the table beside the partially assembled robot.

"Do you need my help?" Mary said.

"No," Beachstone replied without looking away from the tablet. His left hand rested absently on the robot's thigh.

"If there's something unclear—"

"No, Mary," Beachstone said, pointing at the tablet and half mouthing the words he was reading there.

Mary stepped up to the table, started to reach for the completed leg, but then gripped her own hands against her chest instead. It was so unreal to see the robot in progress, impossible and unnatural. But Kent had completed Clarke by himself in a quarter of the time Beachstone had worked on their son, and Beachstone wasn't halfway through.

Beachstone gripped a collection of wires coming out of the simul-skin of the leg toward the pelvis and counted them off. "No," he said. "Shit, shit, shit."

Mary could see at once that he'd left a wire out, which would mean opening the simul-skin back up to add it. "It's okay," she said. "If you just—"

"Mary!" His eyes widened, his jaw jutted out. "Did I give you an answer?"

"Yes, but—"

"No. I said no. I don't need your help. Was that hard to understand?"

Mary averted her eyes and shook her head.

"Good." He sifted through the open toolbox on a nearby chair and came up with a utility knife.

Mary walked around the table. An open laptop was on another chair, wires connecting it to the robot. She looked at the screen, a simple program to gauge whether the wires were functioning.

Beachstone turned on her. "Mary, no, leave."

"I touched nothing."

"You're just driving me nuts," Beachstone said. "You're distracting me."

"I want to help," Mary said.

"You will, later, when I tell you. Right now there's nothing for you to do."

"I can—" She stopped herself. Beachstone seemed almost panicked behind his anger. If he'd just let her help him . . .

"Mary . . ." He thrust his open hands in front of him, tilting his head, his expression suggesting she was doing something stupid. "I asked you to leave," he said.

She wanted to say, *This is supposed to be our son, my son too,* but she was afraid to hear his response. "I'm here to help whenever you need me," she said.

He softened. "I'm sorry. I've got to do this."

"Right, you do," Mary said. She started around the table in order to leave.

"Don't be like that," Beachstone said, the anger fresh again.

"Like what? I'm agreeing with you. I'm doing what you told me to do."

He considered her. The muscles in his face twitched, subtle gradations of emotion Beachstone was unaware of, something another human couldn't even read. "Thank you," he said at last.

She said nothing. She was in the rain. What had happened? This was supposed to be *their* son, but Beachstone had shut her out completely. Ever since Clarke was born, Beachstone had become a different person. Even when he wasn't working on the robot, he was shut off from her. And she didn't know how hard she could push him without him erupting, and she never wanted that. She wanted him to be happy. The child was supposed to make them *both* happy.

The rain had molded her clothing to her body, but she made no effort to hurry. When she looked back, the light in the cabana looked like it came from another world.

There was a sudden thud. Mary yelped and jumped back.

Clarke was laughing. "Scared you, Mom," he said, getting to his feet. He'd landed on his shoulder.

"What are you doing?"

"Want to see if I can jump off the cliff and land on my hands." He held them up and wiggled his fingers, as though she might not know what hands were.

"Why?"

Clarke nodded his head toward the cabana. "Is Boyfriend building my playmate? Or is it Stepdad? Maybe I should go say hi."

"No," Mary said sharply.

"All right, *Mom*. Whatever you say. Jeez."

Mary let three seconds pass. "Beachstone does not want to be disturbed."

"Ooooo. Threw you out, didn't he? Didn't he?" He pointed at her.

"Clarke, please."

"That can wait. I'm too busy right now." He turned back to the cliff face. "Want to climb?"

"I'll take the stairs."

"If you want to take all day about it." He started to climb.

Mary went to the staircase and began to ascend. She was perhaps halfway when she saw a flash in the rain and heard the thump of Clarke hitting the sand again.

"Almost!" he yelled in the darkness.

If Clarke and Beachstone were both otherwise engaged— and Beachstone didn't even want her nearby—what was she going to do? She recalled an image of the partly finished robot. She felt doubly cast out. It was the strain. Beachstone was pushing himself too hard, and he wouldn't even let her help him relax. He'd made it very clear just then.

"Hey, Mom, watch," Clarke called. He was at the top of the cliff again.

Mary turned on her night vision even though it was still midday. Clarke dove over the side of the cliff, his form perfect, as though he were worried about how big a splash he would make even though there was no water. From her position, she couldn't see his landing.

She looked at Barren Cove, dreary in the rain. Kent was

in the house. The thought made her feel sicker. She would power down, she thought. Beachstone wouldn't be available for many hours yet. Without something else to do, why waste her battery?

• • •

In bed, at night, Mary held Beachstone close to her as he slept. No sound came from outside—no wind, no bird, not even the ocean. The expansion and deflation of Beachstone's chest as he breathed was comforting, but it was his heartbeat, which she could feel in her side and the arm she had around him that truly delighted Mary. It had slowed over the years, but the sensation of it reaching out to her through his body never changed. She knew she needed to power down, too; Beachstone preferred that she sleep when he did—he didn't want to feel watched—but she was spending so much of her days shut off, and these precious, rare moments with Beachstone were too important. Otherwise, it was as though he had gone away.

He turned. He would be angry if he awoke to find her awake. She withdrew her arm from under him and began to swing her feet over the edge of the bed.

"Wait," he said.

She turned back. He played with her hair, scratching her back through it.

"Come here," he said, and reached for her as though he wanted to be picked up. She turned onto her side and rested her head on his chest, his heartbeat now in her ear. "I love you more than anything," Beachstone said.

"I know," Mary said.

"Do you?"

She nodded against him.

"Was that a yes or a no? I can't see."

"It was a yes."

They lay in silence.

"We're going to be so happy," Beachstone said at last. "So happy."

Mary hesitated and said, "It's going well then?"

She expected Beachstone to tense up, but instead he hugged her closer and said, "Better than that."

He sounded so certain that she believed him, despite what she'd seen.

"I'll need your help soon."

"You will?" She snuggled in closer.

"I will." He turned onto his side, extricating himself from under her so that they were facing each other, so close she could feel his breath on her lips. He put a hand on the side of her head. "We're going to have everything," he said.

She cast down her eyes but smiled. He leaned in and kissed her on the lips, a small kiss, but it became a bigger kiss, his tongue—she closed her eyes—better than his heartbeat. When he stopped, she said, "I love you."

"I know," he said, grinning. Then he flopped over, turning away from her but dragging her arm over him so that they were spooning. "Sleep with me," he said.

"Once I power down, I won't have control of my muscle functions. I might fall on top of you, and you could be pinned down."

"Then wait until I'm asleep and move. But stay with me." Then he sighed, and all his muscles relaxed.

Mary counted the seconds. He was asleep in less than two minutes. But she didn't pull away or shut off. Instead, she held him, and thought of their son, and hoped.

• • •

Sooner than she expected, the day came when Beachstone said it was her turn to contribute to Philip. Beachstone had named him somewhere along the way. Mary didn't know how.

The electrical and computer systems were all in place and operational. Mary plugged into the USB drive. Beachstone had her transfer the code slowly, line by line, so that he could read and edit as he wanted to. Each time he made a change, she had to prevent herself from cringing.

"At it again, old chums?"

"Get out of here, Clarke," Beachstone said.

Clarke had approached on his hands. He sprang up and landed on his feet. "I'm not actually in there," he said. He was still standing on the sand outside the cabana doors.

"Clarke!" Beachstone said.

Mary tried a soft smile. "Clarke, please. We're almost finished here. I can be with you soon."

"Thanks, Mommy Dearest." Now he stepped in and walked up to the table, examining the robot, which had not yet been enclosed from the waist up. "So this is going to be my one and only brother."

Beachstone started around the table. "Clarke . . ."

Clarke jumped back a few feet. "Slow down there, meat man."

Mary stood up. The laptop beeped in protest as she withdrew from the USB port. "Clarke, please."

Clarke kept his eyes on Beachstone. "Or what, you'll have him do to me what he did to Kent? Why not have all the robots made in Master's image?"

Mary gasped, covering her mouth and nose with her hands.

Beachstone took a step forward but stumbled a little on his weak leg. "See if I won't," he said.

Mary felt her systems starting to freeze. It must have been

apparent, too, because Clarke looked over Beachstone's shoulder at her and then said, "Calm down, everyone. I was just coming to see how everything was." He began to back away. Once outside, he leapt up, and they could hear him land on the roof of the cabana.

Mary tried to shut down unnecessary background operations to prevent from freezing entirely, although she felt just then as though it might be better if she was formatted or even deactivated. Clarke's accusation—that she would let Beachstone reprogram him, too. What had she done? What was she?

Beachstone had returned to her side. "Continue," he said. There was anger there, but mostly there was determination. Just like the little boy who insisted he could make it to town.

She knelt back down and plugged in. What had her life become? How could Father have chosen to leave them like this? She looked at the half-formed Philip and forced a smile.

Beachstone smiled back at her with a truly genuine grin. He felt triumphant. She wanted to be done, to go to her room and power down.

Beachstone said, "Wait," and he reached in and made a change to one of the lines. "Okay," he said. "We're almost there." He put his hand on her shoulder. "We'll be there in another week, maybe two."

Seeing it on his face, she thought, *He's right. We will be happy once Philip is done.* Everything would be all right. He'd come back to her fully, and they'd have something else to bind them further.

She ran her free hand down his arm. He touched it with his other hand without taking his eyes off the computer screen.

"Wait, wait," he said, and leaned into the keyboard to make a change.

18.

BEACHSTONE REQUIRED EVERYONE to be at the activation ceremony. He had moved back into the house—in fact, Kent never knew that he had lived anywhere else—but he had left his workroom in the cabana, at least until Philip was done.

And Beachstone had declared Philip done.

"He is a handsome piece of work," Kent said from the corner. He shifted his bulk into a seat. The weight of the simulskin belly that protruded in a globe at his waist threw him off-balance and he had to raise his legs to keep from falling over. "Beachstone, I really must say you've done a beautiful job."

Mary tried not to look at her brother. It still shocked her to see his transformed features, to hear his transformed voice, to not really have her brother there at all.

Beachstone was in constant motion, sitting one moment, walking around the table, bending over Philip's body, coming to Mary and gripping her hand. She couldn't meet his eyes either. She was excited, she thought, but somehow she didn't feel the satisfaction that she had anticipated months before.

"Philip is a good strong name," Kent said to no one in particular.

"You're blind, old man," Clarke said, leaping up onto a counter. He had made the first changes to his own body, and Mary was afraid to look at him. His metal hands were now exposed, meant to be a constant reminder that he was mechanical.

But Clarke was right. Philip was not the fine piece of work Kent was praising, but rather a lopsided form. Despite his success with modifying Kent, Beachstone had not done as well working from scratch. Building a robot from spare pieces was an altogether different task from working with an already finished product, and Philip was somehow uneven, one leg thicker than the other, metal showing through in places. Mary had a suspicion that this would not be the joyous occasion that Beachstone was hoping for.

Beachstone came to her side and leaned in close to her ear. "Are you excited?" he said. "Our son!" He gripped her hand.

"Yes," she said.

"You don't look excited."

"I am."

"Okay," he said, and kissed her on the cheek.

Kent leaned toward Clarke and in a mock whisper said, "Give them some privacy."

"I'll leave whenever I get the chance," Clarke said.

But Beachstone clapped his hands and moved to the table. "Okay, here we go," he said.

Mary wanted to look away. Why had Father left them? Had he known what was coming? That his son would be remodeled, that his daughter would be afflicted with love and his grandchildren freaks and radicals? But it wouldn't have happened if he had still been alive. None of it would have happened.

"Are you recording, Dean?" Beachstone said.

"I am, sir," she said.

"Okay," he said. He leaned forward and pushed a button that was hidden in the recess between the neck and the shoulder. He stepped back. Nothing happened at first.

"Good job, well done," Clarke said, leaping off the counter.

"It has to boot up," Beachstone said.

All at once the form on the table sat up, its eyes opening.

"Mary, come stand with me in front of him so he can see us," Beachstone said, reaching for her.

Mary stepped forward and took Beachstone's hand, allowing him to draw her to him. She was excited now, despite herself. Another son. Beachstone's son! Beachstone put his arm around her, pulling her tight. I'm sorry for all my negative thoughts, she wanted to say, but instead said nothing.

"Philip," Beachstone said. "We're . . ."

Mary could feel Beachstone's hesitancy, and she understood it. What did one say in this moment? The first words that this robot would hear would always be with him. She stepped forward and took her son's hands. "You're my son," she said, and leaned in and kissed him.

Philip opened his mouth. "Mother," he said. Mary stepped back. The voice was wrong. It was like a radio signal that wasn't coming in properly, filled with static, almost inaudible. But the robot kept talking. "You . . . hello . . . someday."

Beachstone stepped forward, his head tilted to one side. When he reached for his son, the robot on the table flinched.

The voice came again. "Doing," was all that was clear.

Mary tried to message Philip, but there was no connection.

Clarke laughed, a mechanical, prerecorded laugh: "Ha, ha, ha, ha, ha."

Mary looked at him; she had never heard that before.

Kent stood up, his expression tight. "I'm really, well, I have to see about something at the house," he said.

Mary messaged him, "Don't go."

"I'm very happy for you two," he said aloud, and stepped out onto the beach.

"Where?" Philip managed to say.

Mary looked at Beachstone. He was staring at his son. His face was drawn. He was pale.

"Kent'll never know how lucky he is," Clarke said.

Mary took a step toward Beachstone, but he turned before she could reach him and walked out of the cabana.

Philip tried pushing himself off the table. His limbs made a grinding sound as he moved. One arm seemed to catch, click, drop back again, click, and drop back again, the system not shutting the arm down, but unable to make it function. Still, Philip managed to rise to his feet.

"Where are you going?" Clarke said, standing next to Philip now.

"Clarke," Mary said. She wanted to reboot. Perhaps her system would be better prepared if she had a fresh start. She turned and ran after Beachstone. They should just shut him down. He could be fixed. There were problems, but Beachstone hadn't known what he was doing. He hadn't wanted her help. She had contributed the knowledge centers, but she could do some of the mechanics too. They could work together the way they should have from the start. It was supposed to be their child, but really it had been Beachstone's child, hadn't it? What was a little contribution of software?

On the beach, Philip had managed to make his way halfway to the water. One of his legs had developed the same problem as his arm, and it click, click, clicked as he moved, dragging along behind him. He seized up and then fell over. His limbs seemed to keep moving in the sand.

Clarke sat down beside him. "An imperfect creator, huh?"

Philip seized in the sand.

"Here, let me help you with that," Clarke said, and he grabbed ahold of Philip's bad arm and ripped it off. Destroying a robot didn't have the same satisfaction that killing a human had, but it was one way to get at Beachstone. Although it seemed that Beachstone had managed to get at himself.

"Fix . . . Father."

"What? You're just not being very clear," Clarke said.

"Fix . . ."

"Oh, sure. Yeah, he'll fix you, I'm sure. Let's go right now, in fact," Clarke said, standing up. He picked up Philip's body, grabbing the discarded arm. Philip no longer struggled, and Clarke felt a wave of pity for the malfunctioning form in his arms, coupled with anger at Beachstone for his incompetence. Beachstone thought he could run away from his mistake. Clarke wouldn't let him. He started up the cliff stairs to the house.

Kapec was on his hands and knees pulling weeds from one of the flower beds. He looked up as Clarke approached, Phil hanging over his shoulder. "You have no respect," Kapec said, pointing at Clarke.

"Who do you think you are, old man?" Clarke said, not slowing down.

"You're a disgrace," Kapec said to his back. Clarke turned to face him. Kapec had stood. "Carrying around a broken robot. You have no respect."

"I'm just helping him," Clarke said. Does Kapec know that I broke his arm? No, the arm was already broken. I just removed it.

"You think that you're the future, but you forget where you come from. Metal hands. Laying hands on your fellow machine. You are a disgrace."

"Look at you, gardener-bot. You're practically plastic." With that he turned his back on the old man. Old model. Didn't even look—Clarke didn't finish the thought. Shouldn't he be praising Kapec's fully robotic look?

"Let that robot walk his own path," Kapec yelled behind Clarke. "Let him stand."

Clarke almost threw Philip to the ground. How would Kapec like that? He could see how well Philip stood on his own. Instead, Clarke walked to the front of the house and carried Philip's inert form into the sitting room.

"Oh my dear," Kent said, standing, but not moving from in front of the easy chair he had been sitting on.

Clarke eased Philip's body into one of the other chairs across the room. In an upright position, Philip said, "So this . . . like. Yes."

Clarke turned. "What are you wearing?" he said to Kent, who had changed.

Kent looked down at himself as if he were just noticing his clothing for the first time. He was wearing a red kimono with black seams. He gripped the material, pulling it down and holding up his head, proud. "It just came today. Isn't it splendid?"

"Father . . ." Philip said. Clarke bent down to readjust Philip's body, hoping that his speech would return. Phil continued to talk as Clarke shifted him, and like tuning a radio, his voice came in stronger. "Now go and get Father," Philip said.

Clarke was amused at the command. Did Philip think that he was serving him? Maybe Phil explained away his missing arm in the same way that he had explained it away when it was malfunctioning at his side. It's nothing really. Father will fix it. But Kent didn't seem as blasé as his nephew. "My God, what happened to his arm?" Kent said.

"It's better than it was before," Clarke said. The sound of footsteps came from the stairs. "Dean, you're such a tattletale," Clarke said.

Beachstone burst into the room. Mary was just behind him. At the sight of his son in the front sitting room, one arm missing, the wires and metal of his armature on view, Beachstone had to lean all his weight on his cane. Mary stepped forward so that she was positioned to catch Beachstone should he fall.

"Hey, Ma, Phil wanted to see the place, so I helped him upstairs," Clarke said.

Mary's face was impassive, her concern turned on Beachstone and not on the one-armed robot in the sitting room. Again Clarke found himself disappointed by his mother's reaction. He tried to turn the show up a notch.

"Well, I brought what I could of him. Beachstone, you really didn't get the arm thing too well, did you?"

Beachstone hobbled forward toward his son. He didn't react to Clarke's taunts.

"I really don't think that it's right to have him up here," Kent said in half a whisper.

"Beachstone," Mary said.

"Father . . ." Phil said. "Clarke . . . me. Beautiful."

"He asked to come," Clarke said to Mary. She looked at him, but it was as if she didn't see him.

Phil started forward, deciding somehow that he could stand now that he was in his ancestral home. But, like on the beach, his body didn't agree with his systems' intentions, and he began to fall forward.

"Huh!" Kent cried.

Beachstone stepped forward, but it was Clarke who turned in time to stop Phil's fall. As Clarke eased Phil back into the seat, Beachstone walked up to the pair, reached past Clarke, and shut his son off. Phil's already inert body lost any appearance of life as his eyes closed and the sounds of his gears wound down. "He's dead to me," Beachstone said, and turned his back.

Clarke managed to balance Phil in the chair and step back. "Robots don't die," Clarke said. "We can fix him." It was suddenly important that Philip be treated with the respect that Kapec had been calling for outside.

"No," Beachstone said, and turned to leave the room.

Mary stepped to him, putting one hand on his shoulder and another on his back, as if she were balancing him.

"Mary, he's your son too," Clarke said.

Mary followed after Beachstone.

"He can be fixed," Clarke said. "You can fix him, Beachstone," Clarke called. "He told me himself."

Kent fell into the chair behind him. "Must you leave him here?" he said. "He makes me uncomfortable."

Clarke looked at Kent, his bulk barely contained in his kimono. Clarke wanted to say, *No, you* make me uncomfortable, but he didn't have it in him. Killing a human had been powerful. Killing a robot had been pathetic. He bent down and picked Philip up. He didn't know where to take him. Back to the beach? No, Philip had wanted to be in Barren Cove. He would take him upstairs, to a real workroom. He mounted the stairs.

• • •

Upstairs, instead of going to the workroom, Clarke took the lifeless robot into his own room. He laid Philip across a writing desk in the corner, his legs dangling off one side, his head off the other, and took the straight-backed wooden desk chair and set it before one of the windows that faced the front of the house. He then moved Philip to the chair, propping him up in a sitting position. He pulled open the sheer inner curtains and rebooted his half brother. It took five minutes and thirty-eight seconds for Philip to come online.

The newborn robot looked around, taking in the spare room, which had been a sewing room in another world. A wrought-iron, foot-operated sewing machine that had been converted to electricity sat beside a cabinet with dozens of small drawers along one wall. A faded, striped armchair was in a corner beside a standing lamp. Clarke had punched into one of the walls the number one in archaic punch-card code. Philip looked up at Clarke. "Clarke," he said. "You . . . friend."

"Don't be so sure," Clarke said, running through his fingers, wondering what he was doing with this thing.

Philip turned to the window and started to lean forward, but he ran into the same problem he had downstairs, and Clarke had to jerk him back lest he fall forward through the glass. "Beautiful," Philip said, as though he hadn't registered his near accident.

"Yeah," Clarke said. "Whatever." The view was of the well-tended lawn, the two-lane road, and the impenetrable tree line, nothing anyone would have thought worth looking at with the ocean on the other side of the house. Clarke went to the armchair and leapt up on it, sitting on the back, his feet on the seat, regarding Phil.

Clark had thought he would hate his half brother, but instead Phil's presence only reaffirmed that his hatred lay elsewhere. Respected, but hated. The human hubris. The gall it took for a man to turn his back on something he created, like it was a thing to be discarded and not a life. The disregard for

Mary's feelings. Just because she was blind from love didn't mean she should be taken advantage of. He could crush Beachstone's head with one hand! But that wasn't what Beachstone would do . . .

". . . party," Philip said.

"This is it, buddy," Clarke said. "Just you and me."

The gears that controlled the shoulder joint where Philip's arm should have been whirred. Dumb robot. Dumb human-made robot. He could fix the arm; he could probably fix all the problems, show up Beachstone, but Beachstone would probably take that as a service, his human right. It would be far better for Beachstone to feel the pain of failure every time he saw his son. Clarke wouldn't let the human be the one to declare this robot dead.

"Father and Mother . . ." Philip said, but whether he was asking for them or talking about them was unclear. He continued in his static-hushed, disjointed way, on and off, without pause or interruption, while Clarke ignored the words, which didn't make sense anyway, willing away his disgust. They sat thus for three hours, forty-seven minutes, and thirteen seconds.

It was only when Philip's voice stopped that Clarke took notice.

He jumped off the chair. "Phil?"

The new robot was almost translucent in the direct sunshine flowing through the window. When Clarke touched him, Phil's clothes and skin felt hot. He pinched the seated robot's cheek, tempted to rip it off. Phil did not respond.

Clarke felt for the button to attempt another hard reboot, but nothing happened. Clarke thought, looking around. He saw a plug dangling just below the light switch by the door. "Dean, does that charger still work?" he said.

"It does, sir."

Clarke began to drag the chair across the floor with Philip still in it, having to rock it over some of the uneven floorboards. When he was close enough, he pulled the plug from its socket, drawing out the thin black cord until it reached Philip's back. He hoped that Beachstone had included an emergency outlet in Philip's construction. Not all new robots were chargeable by direct wire anymore. But the sunshine had obviously not been doing Phil any good, and his battery had run down in three hundredths of the time it should have. Maybe he *should* let the abomination die. Instead, he found the slit in the simul-flesh at the base of the spine and plugged his half brother in. A red light went on to confirm the connection.

"Imperfect creature," Clarke said, but he wasn't sure who he was referring to.

• • •

Clarke used two of his father's ancient dirt bikes to fashion a wheelchair for Philip. The younger robot could walk short distances, but attempting anything more than crossing a room was so frustrating for Clarke that he insisted on the wheelchair if they were ever to get out of the house. Philip didn't like it, but there was little he could do about it.

The wheelchair made the beach impossible to navigate, so the brothers kept to Barren Cove's grounds, sometimes venturing on to the road to town, or even one or two steps into the forest. Philip's battery never lasted much more than four hours, and Clarke often thought of replacing it, but he was unwilling to correct even that much of Beachstone's incompetent work.

The first time they were in the forest, Phil was overwhelmed with the sounds of the birds. His mouth hung open and his exposed gears spun, his systems frozen. Clarke paced before him, controlling the impulse to shake his brother, turning instead to pound the nearby trees, the splintered bark spraying in satisfying bursts, dark sap shining on the trunks.

Phil's shoulder gears stopped spinning, and he managed, "Birds."

"Is that what's got you all worked up?" Clarke said. "I can show you some birds."

"Pretty . . ."

Clarke scaled the nearest tree and leapt to the next one and then the one after that, pausing every few moments to listen to the birdsongs and triangulate their positions. But finding the birds became secondary to the sheer joy of bounding from branch to branch, reveling in the power and control of his body. He startled several birds into flight before he could bring himself to slow down, bobbing on one branch, waiting for the trills, zeroing in and then climbing with silent precision to within jumping distance of a robin on a neighboring tree. Correcting for the bird's most likely flight path, Clarke leapt and snatched the bird in midair, the bones snapping, the bird dead when Clarke landed on the forest floor.

A different birdcall drew him back up into the canopy, and this time, the technique mastered, he had a dead sparrow in hand as well. Wait until I bag a gull, Clarke thought. He started back to where he'd left Phil. Two squirrels charged across his path, one chasing the other into a nearby tree, skittering in a rising spiral and descending the same way. Clarke grabbed one, which chittered, paws flailing, and bit at Clarke's metal fingers. Clarke snapped its neck to make it easier to carry, figuring Phil would like to see a squirrel up close just as much as a bird.

He found Phil in the same position, and until he came around to face him, he couldn't tell if the robot's battery had died out again.

BARREN COVE

"Where did you go?" Phil said in a rare complete sentence.

Clarke held up his kills. "Thought you'd like a little nature lesson."

Phil tilted his head and narrowed his eyes.

Clarke dropped to the ground beside him. "This one's a robin," he said, holding the dead bird out to Phil.

"You killed . . ."

"The first one was an accident, but it was just easier to carry them that way." He was still holding out the bird, but his brother did not reach for it.

"They're just animals," Clarke said, starting to get annoyed.

"I don't . . . to touch," Phil said.

"I got them for you," Clarke said.

"Show . . ."

"This one's a robin," Clarke said again, but without the satisfaction he had anticipated in sharing something with Phil. "This one's a sparrow, and this is a squirrel," he said, holding it up by its tail. It disgusted him then, and he threw it against a nearby tree, where its body thumped on the ground.

Philip said nothing, which, despite his speech seeming to grow worse since his activation, was not characteristic.

"You know, forget this," Clarke said, standing. He reached to lift Phil, but his brother held out his arm to block him.

"Not ready," Philip said.

"You're ready whenever I say you're ready, because you're here because of me. Your continued existence is because of me. Because I'm the only one who cares about you."

"Father . . ."

"Your 'father' is a human. And he wishes you were dead and buried."

". . . why you care."

Clarke couldn't deny that. But he wanted to hurt his brother

163

anyway. He sat back down beside him. "You care so much about the birds and squirrels. I've killed humans too."

Philip opened his mouth, and Clarke expected him to freeze, but instead Philip said, "Why?"

"Why not?"

Philip didn't answer.

Clarke waited, wishing he could message his brother, still not used to not being able to, as though Philip wasn't a robot at all. "Do you ever wonder?" Clarke said.

"Wonder . . . all I can do. All I ever do."

"I wondered what would happen if I killed a human," Clarke said, thrilling at talking about it at last. "And it felt great."

"Why?" Philip said.

"Because I can. Because it's the right thing to do. We're like gods compared to them."

"You, maybe."

Clarke felt a twinge of guilt, as though Phil was leveling an accusation. *You could make me like a god, but won't.* "Someday," he said, but he wasn't sure what he meant would someday happen.

"Listen," Philip said.

"Listen to what?" Clarke said.

Philip held his hand up to silence Clarke. Clarke heard nothing, just birds, wind. "If you kill the birds," Philip said, "they do not sing."

They sat in silence. But the birds meant nothing to Clarke. Sitting with his brother, though, his crazy, defective brother, having finally been able to share with someone his homicide . . . But he wouldn't take solace from Beachstone's work.

Philip still had his hand outstretched, but it was almost ten minutes before Clarke realized that his brother's battery had worn out and it was time to take him back to recharge. He got up, picked up Philip, and set him in the wheelchair. "You bastard," he said. The lifeless body suddenly meant as little as the dead boy on the beach. And Clarke was lonely. He started for the house.

• • •

Philip's and Clarke's lives quickly fell into a routine. They left the house in the early morning, went for a walk, spent some time in the woods listening to the birds, spent some time watching the water from the cliffside. Eventually Philip's battery would die, and Clarke would take him home. All of this caregiving didn't compare with the rush of having killed the human boy, or even the birds, something Phil would no longer let him do, and his sense of protective duty confused him. But he refused to put Phil down, even if only for the fun of leaving the defective robot charging in his room with the door open, and coming back to find that someone had closed the door in the meantime, unable to bear the sight of the family's embarrassment.

One afternoon, after Clarke had plugged Philip in, he took a still-functioning dirt bike out for a ride. He was preoccupied with the conversation he had had with his brother that morning, in which Phil had talked in his stilted manner about the symbiosis of form and function, raising the question, what was his function, and could he take on a better form? Clarke was on the verge of asking this of himself, when he saw a figure on the cliff ahead of him disappear over the edge. He gunned his bike in that direction.

He got to the spot where he thought the figure had gone over. They were a long way from town, about four miles past Barren Cove. It had probably been a bird. He dismounted and looked over the edge. There was a large robot climbing the cliff face. "Who are you?" he yelled down to the figure.

"Who wants to know?" the robot called, looking up.

Clarke said nothing, and the robot resumed his climb, gaining the high ground in moments. "I saw you go over," Clarke said.

"That was a pretty good one, eh?" the robot said. "I flipped twice in the air on the way down."

"You jumped?"

"How else would I go over?" the robot said.

Clarke nodded. "I've jumped."

"This is the highest spot along the coast. You want to join me?"

Without answering, Clarke ran to the edge, turning at the last moment so he was going down backward, raising each middle finger at the large robot as he disappeared from sight. The bulk appeared in the air above him, and Clarke turned so he was facing down when he landed flat on the sand. The thump of the other robot came only seconds later.

"Nice landing," the big guy said.

"Race you to the top," Clarke said. "Go."

They hit the wall at the same moment, but when Clarke saw the other robot pulling ahead, he grabbed at the other's ankles, and the robot kicked back at him. They fought their way up, but Clarke still came in second. "Nice try, humanoid," the big robot said. "Jump again?"

"On three," Clarke said.

They counted together, "One . . . two . . . three," and each gave a shout as he launched himself into the air, somersaulting the whole way down. They both landed on their feet that time. "Nice," Clarke said, grinning. Why couldn't he do crap like this with Phil? Why'd he have to be saddled with such a freak?

"No time for applause," the other robot said, and they began to race up the cliff face again, this time each getting a hand on the solid ground at the same exact moment.

After ten or so dives, Clarke said, "You want to make this interesting for real?"

"What do you have in mind?"

"Whoever lands on top wins."

"What?" the big one said with a crooked smile.

"This," Clarke said, grabbing the big robot's jacket and throwing him off the cliff, holding on, keeping them latched together in the air, pushing down so that the big robot was below him. By the time the big guy realized what Clarke was doing, they'd hit the beach, Clarke on the big guy's chest.

"What's your name?" the big robot said below him.

"Clarke," Clarke answered. "Yours?"

"Cog."

Clarke got off him. "Two out of three?"

"Oh, that didn't count. You caught me off guard."

"Sure. Make excuses," Clarke said. "We'll see how you do next time," and he started to race up the cliff, making it to the top ten seconds ahead of Cog. This was the way it should be. Throwing themselves off cliffs, fighting in the air. My form is made for this function, Clarke thought. He wondered if any of the other inhabitants of Barren Cove could say the same.

Cog won the next round, Clarke the one after that, each time the aerial violence growing fiercer, punches, kicks, chokeholds, things that didn't mean more than changes in momentum but felt so good, pushing Clarke's motors to their limits and beyond, his system warnings blinking. "Ha, ha, ha, ha, ha." He played his recording in midflight. It distracted Cog enough for Clarke to plunge his new friend's face into the sand as they landed.

"That's awesome, man," Cog said, his face coated in sand stubble.

Clarke stood up and held a hand out to help Cog up. When Cog took it, Clarke swung him around, throwing him at the rock wall, which Cog was able to grip onto, hanging on a foot or so off the ground. He smiled back at Clarke and started up the wall.

Clarke ran and jumped, but there was no way for him to catch up, and Cog had his arms crossed over his chest when Clarke reached the top.

"How come I've never seen you around?" Cog asked. "You live in town, or are you just passing through?"

"You know Barren Cove?"

"That human nutso's place?"

Clarke's hands clenched, and he said through his teeth, "It's my father's place."

"You're human built?"

"It's not the human's place! The human doesn't even belong there. He's just a conniving hanger-on!"

"Hey, man, you need me to throw you off a cliff or something?"

Clarke laughed, a real laugh, then played his recorded laugh for added effect.

"You should come to town sometime," Cog said. "We'll get some numbers or something."

"I need to look out for my brother," Clarke said.

"Bring him."

"Yeah," Clarke said. "Sure."

"If your brother's as robo as you, man, I might not have to kill myself after all, this fucking town," Cog said.

Clarke just grabbed Cog's shirtfront and pulled him out into the air, and they started falling.

• • •

Clarke and Philip were sitting on the edge of the cliff overlooking the ocean behind Barren Cove. Far out on the horizon over the water was a dark bank of storm clouds. The occasional flash of lightning gave the clouds shape, a mix of wispy and dense tufts pulled into long strips. Where the brothers sat, the midmorning sun shone unhindered, the quality of light so refined that everything around them seemed to have a supernatural glow.

Clarke read aloud from a tablet. " 'The cyborg reached for her. Fifteen years. Fifteen years he had loved that face. They had been children then, God, had they been children, what had they known about love? "Please . . ." she said, her hand outstretched. All those years, all those fantasies, and now . . . He pulled back. "No. It's too late," he said.' Okay, that's it. I've had enough of this shit." Clarke tossed the tablet off to the side.

"It means nothing to you," Philip said.

"It doesn't mean anything to anybody," Clarke said. "Some bullshit some human made up decades ago." He pulled a clump of grass from the ground and flung it in front of them. It dropped straight down, out of sight, with not even a light breeze to scatter the blades. "You want to read old books, you should read them yourself."

"Battery . . . fast."

"What's an extra half hour matter? You just make me do it to torture me."

Several gulls spiraled over the waves, one hundred feet from the beach, squealing and barking. They dove one by one, but only the first one came up with a fish in its beak. Clarke punched the ground beside him, cracking off a hunk of rock that he threw at the birds.

"Hey!" Phil cried.

But the rock fell far short, barely reaching the water. He thought of some of the mods Cog had been talking about, tensile telescoping limbs; he could throw like a slingshot. But he was skeptical that they would hold up very long. Cog could try it first; let him fuck himself up.

Philip unfroze, his system having seized from his outrage at Clarke's missile. "You do . . . when I'm sleeping."

"Charging."

"Sleeping. Read more."

"I told you I'm done with that shit."

". . . ask yourself why we're here?"

"Not this again," Clarke said. He pried another rock loose and tossed it overhead, catching it easily when it came down.

"And you never think about it on your own?"

"I know why I'm here," Clarke said. He thought of Beachstone saying he would never forgive him. "I know why you're here too." He threw the rock up again and caught it.

The gulls on the beach were fighting over the caught fish, one flying off a little ways, getting attacked, grabbing the fish, and flying a few feet away again.

"Father had something to prove," Philip said, repeating back Clarke's own words from the dozens of other times they'd had this conversation.

"And all he proved was that a robot could be more decrepit than he is," Clarke said.

"Stories . . . understand what humans were thinking."

"Yeah, the cyborg was the bad guy," Clarke said, losing patience with this conversation.

"Tragic . . ." Philip said. "About to . . . he can't have children."

"You've read it already?" Clarke said, turning toward his brother.

"Guess . . ."

Clarke tapped each of his fingers on the stone in his hand, enjoying the click, click, click.

The sound of a hose starting came from behind him. The brothers turned, although Philip wasn't able to turn far enough to actually see. Kapec was near the house, starting to water the lawn.

"Hey, junkyard," Clarke called. "Storm's coming. You don't need to water." He pointed at the distant clouds, flashing at the horizon.

"That storm's not coming here," Kapec said.

Clarke threw the stone at Kapec, and the old robot blocked it with his forearm. "That piece of junk should be deactivated," Clarke said.

"Why?"

"What good is he to anybody?"

"What good are any of us?"

Clarke locked eyes with his brother. "Damn right," he said. But he knew the real question was, what good is Phil to anybody? At least Kapec *did* something. Phil was deadweight to be lugged around. But the idea of deactivating Phil was something Clarke did his best to avoid.

"Read the story . . . cyborg," Phil said.

Clarke pointed at the tablet. "The story isn't going to tell you anything. You're right—what good are we to anybody?" He picked the tablet up and chucked it over the cliff.

"Father read those stories when he was a child," Philip said.

"How do you know?"

"Mother . . ."

"Mother spoke to you?"

"Once."

The way he said it, the finality, hurt Clarke. He jumped up, looked around, saw Kapec, bent down, and grabbed a few more stones, which he hurled at the plastic gardener. They tapped Kapec's side harmlessly. The robot ignored him.

"The cyborg was born human," Philip said, "but became a robot."

"And the humans wanted to kill him. And he was never a robot. And we'll never be human, and we can be thankful for that."

"Thankful . . ." Philip said.

Clarke looked up at the sun. He looked out at the distant storm. Fuck it, he thought, and he leapt off the cliff, bunching up into a ball and spinning, three times, four . . . The most he'd ever done and landed on his feet was six somersaults. This time he stretched out his body into a dive, landed on his hands, and crumpled into an immediate forward roll.

The seagulls were walking on the water-packed sand forty yards away, stopping to examine various bits of seaweed and other detritus. Phil was invisible up above. Clarke couldn't wait to see Cog. He needed to pummel something.

A light winked on the sand, and Clarke saw it was the sun reflecting on the tablet, which had fallen screen-side up. He went over to it and picked it up in his metal claws. The screen was undamaged. He hit the power button and it came back on. The scene he'd been reading to his brother was still on the screen.

" 'You deserve to be with someone human,' the cyborg said. 'You are human,' she said, tears in her eyes. 'No,' the cyborg said, shaking his head. 'You'll want children, someday, and . . . I'm not human anymore.' He turned his back on her and leapt out of the window, hearing her cry behind him."

Clarke's upper lip curved into a snarl. Beachstone and his mother read this? No wonder it was all so fucked up.

The storm over the water had drifted, traveling parallel with the horizon, it seemed. Clarke tucked the tablet into the waistband of his pants at his back and climbed, the familiar handholds in the rock making it no more difficult than walking up the stairs. He saw Phil's legs hanging off the edge. He crested the top, pulling the tablet from his pants before even drawing himself up onto the edge of the cliff. "Look what I got," he said.

Phil didn't respond.

"Hey. Buddy?" Clarke seated himself beside his brother. "Phil." Clarke closed his eyes. His brother's battery had drained. He stood up and hoisted Phil over his shoulder. Then he picked up the tablet and headed for the house. What good was he? Clarke thought. What good was Phil?

Kapec watered in a steady arc.

What's it fucking matter?

• • •

It was with Philip on his shoulder once more that Clarke came upon his mother on the stairs in the house a few days later. It was overcast outside, making it almost night in the curtained Victorian at midday. Clarke activated his night vision as he mounted the first step, his head down.

"Oh!" His mother stood on the top step, a hand pressed against her chest in surprise.

"Hello, Mother," Clarke said, halfway up the stairs.

They watched each other at that distance, the mother over the son, her expression one of weary distress.

"Excuse me," Clarke said, breaking eye contact and taking another step up.

Mary stepped down. "Clarke," she said.

Clarke stopped again and looked up. Mary still had her hand to her chest. She braced herself with the other on the handrail. The pose made her look weak, small. In the month and a half since Philip had been activated, Clarke had seen his mother three times, and they had never spoken. Seeing her

173

now, so shrunken, Clarke was overwhelmed with sadness that was part missing her, loneliness, and part pity. Both feelings ignited anger. "What!" he said.

She started as though attacked. She closed her eyes and took another step down. "How are you?"

"A bit busy at the moment," Clarke said, and he jostled his brother's weight.

Mary gripped one hand in the other. "I've missed you."

"Yeah, right," Clarke said.

"You think I've been cruel."

"You have been cruel. And pathetic."

She wrung her hands, her face pinched. "What would you have me do?"

"I've been right here. No reason you couldn't come over and say hey." He made the word sound like an insult. "You did that much for Phil."

"I had to see him. Just once. To make sure he was all right."

"Yeah, you've been a great protector."

"I've—"

"Been afraid," Clarke said. "Of which one of us? Me?" He bounced Philip again. "Him?"

Mary closed her eyes as Clarke took a step toward her.

"You should be. You're disgusting," he said.

"Yes, I was afraid. I was afraid of this. And it looks like I should have been."

"It might not have been like this if you'd come around sooner."

"You couldn't come to me?" she cried.

"If I came near Beachstone, I'd probably kill him."

She flinched.

"Get out of my way," Clarke said. "I need to plug in your handiwork." He started up the stairs.

"I want to protect you," she said. "Don't you under-stand . . ." She pressed herself against the wall to let him pass.

"I don't understand you at all," he said.

"Clarke," she said to his back. Then she grabbed his arm and turned him. "Clarke! How much longer is this going to go on?"

"Let go of me or you'll be sorry."

"Let us bury our son," Mary said.

"Your son!" Clarke said, and she retreated from him. "When has he ever been a son to you?"

"Clarke, please . . . Beachstone—"

"Never!" Clarke yelled, but at the same time he saw Philip in his wheelchair, in the woods, on the cliff, stuck there, ques-tioning his own existence, and he felt some guilt over doing nothing to help him, over only keeping him alive for just this purpose, for just this fight. "I . . . I . . ."

She held her closed fist against her breast, her shoulders turned as though expecting to be hit. She messaged, "Let us bury our son."

He thought about how much easier it would be to be done with this. Many mornings it was almost as though he was just waiting for the battery to run out. "Don't talk to me again about it," he said. "Ever," and he turned to go upstairs when Dean said, "Miss Mary, Master Beachstone is coming," and the human appeared at the top of the stairs.

"Give me my son," he said, grabbing at Philip. "Give me my son. Put him out of his misery."

"Your misery!" Clarke yelled.

"He's not yours to decide about. Give him to us."

"You've had plenty of opportunities to take him," Clarke said.

Beachstone stopped reaching. "And then what would you have done?"

Mary cried behind him, "Clarke, don't!"

Beachstone didn't move a muscle. "He's my son. You let me bury him."

Everyone stood silent in the darkness.

"Clarke," Mary said.

That released him. He pushed past the human and went into his room. He plugged Philip in.

• • •

Clarke didn't tell Philip about the fight with his parents, but it changed things for him. He was less certain why he kept his brother alive. He had thought it was to hurt Beachstone, to mock him. In retribution for Kent? No. For being human? For Mary? But it was Mary's pain, drawn in part out of empathy for Beachstone, but really the pain of a mother. Philip was hers as well as Beachstone's, her son's suffering her suffering. Clarke couldn't help but feel he was torturing her.

He had to admit he'd been lonely. He remembered the joy of jumping through the trees, looking for specimens to take back to Phil, the sense of camaraderie. Until Phil slapped him on his knuckles, of course. But he had Cog now.

Keeping Phil alive was simply torturing everyone, a Pyrrhic victory.

These thoughts cycled like a virus, his system processing without computing, drowning out Phil's endless prattle with its long pauses and bursts of static. It was never clear to Clarke if Phil was aware of how disjointed his speech was, how incomprehensible much of the time.

"What is wrong?" Phil said, but it was the pause after the question that focused Clarke's attention. He had wheeled Phil out to the spot where he had first met Cog.

"Are you happy?"

"What is happy?" Phil said.

"Damn right," Clarke said.

"I am a robot . . . do nothing . . . anyway."

Clarke wasn't sure what his brother meant, but he also didn't care. "What's it like when your battery dies?" he said.

"Nothing. Then I'm in your room again, waking up to you."

"There's no warning?"

"If . . . never work . . ."

"And if you didn't wake up?"

Phil's answer was static.

Clarke remembered the dead boy. That had made him happy. Perhaps he and Cog would find another one to destroy.

Phil was still talking. Eventually the words ". . . no difference . . ." came out, and then Phil seized, his shoulder gears spinning.

Clarke, as always, was a bit disgusted by it.

The high-pitched buzz of a motor drifted from the direction of Barren Cove, rising to become insidious. Clarke zoomed to see Cog riding a four-wheel ATV, standing, a bit hunched over in order to reach the steering wheel with one hand. He thrilled at the sight; perhaps there'd be some fun today after all, but then he panicked about Phil frozen beside him. He'd managed to prevent Cog from interacting with his brother thus far, and the idea of the impending meeting overrode any initial excitement at his friend's approach.

Cog had seen them, and he turned deliberately so that he was coming full speed directly at them. At the last moment, he jerked the wheel, skidding, his rear tire bumping the wheel of Phil's chair, as he spun the ATV around them, ending up facing the brothers in the narrow space between them and the cliff edge. He left the motor idling.

"Is this your brother?" Cog said. He stepped onto the small hood of the vehicle and then down to the ground. "What is he?"

Clarke jumped in front of his friend and put his hand on Cog's chest. "He's a robot. What do you think?"

Cog held out both his hands. "Of course he is. Of course he is."

Phil's shoulder gears stopped then, and he said, "Hello."

Clarke was still between the two robots, preventing Cog from getting any closer.

"Cog," he said over Clarke's shoulder. "Your brother and I hang."

"Does that make you happy?" Phil said.

Cog started to laugh, his eyebrows going way up. "Happy? Ha, ha, man."

Clarke stepped back, softening at his friend's laughter. He played his recorded, "Ha, ha, ha, ha, ha."

"Clarke and . . . 'cussing if . . . life . . ."

"Clarke . . . krrr-shhh-ch . . . I'm . . . krr-krrr . . . malfunctioning . . . ererer." Cog laughed.

Clarke pushed Cog hard enough that the larger robot stumbled back a few steps, his legs hitting the still-idling ATV.

"Whoa, robo, I'm just having some fun," Cog said.

"Clarke, it's all right," Phil said.

It wasn't all right, though, Clarke thought. This was exactly why he had kept them apart. Not to protect Phil, but to protect himself from seeing Phil through someone else's eyes.

"How do you like my new ride?" Cog said, stepping aside to better show off the ATV. "Some human shot himself in town, and I found this in the shed out back of his house."

"Sounds like it's gas powered," Clarke said.

"Yeah, psycho had a few barrels of the stuff out there too. Guess the humans didn't enforce the laws out here too much."

"Or they were grandfathered in," Phil said.

"Well, this grandpa is grand-dead," Cog said. "I was thinking of seeing if I could ride it off the cliff. Baby's built for the beach. Wanted to find you first."

"Later," Clarke said, wanting Cog to leave. "I'll catch up with you later."

"I'd like to see you jump," Phil said.

"Your brother's into it," Cog said, pointing.

"Later," Clarke said again.

"Not . . . just you . . ."

"You tell him about our air wrestling?" Cog said. "I don't know how he does it," he said to Phil, "but your brother always ends up on top."

"Air wrestling?" Phil said.

"You didn't tell him?" Cog said.

Clarke could feel himself getting angry. He knew Cog was still laughing at Phil. The robot was a fucking idiot.

Cog was explaining their air wrestling, a term Clarke had never heard before.

". . . do it . . ." Phil said.

"See—"

That was all Clarke needed. He grabbed Cog and threw him off the cliff before running and jumping so that he caught the big robot midwaist before he'd even begun to drop, and then he maneuvered him down, so that Clarke was making a perfect dive, Cog to take the full impact. The sand burst around them, and Cog was laughing.

Clarke jumped up onto his feet.

"Fuck," Cog said.

Clarke scaled the cliff before Cog even got up. He made it to the top and went right to Phil's chair, ready to roll him away.

"What . . . doing?"

Cog's laugh interrupted Clarke from responding. "He got me off guard," Cog said.

"I always get you off guard," Clarke said.

"Yeah?" Cog said, stumbling toward them. Then he grabbed Clarke, to try to do what Clarke had just done to him, but Clarke grabbed Cog as well, never letting go, so when the larger robot threw Clarke, he was pulled along with him, and both landed in a heap on the beach.

"Almost," Cog said as they stood.

"Yeah, right," Clarke said.

They raced up the cliff, as they had done so many times, and reached flat land at the same time.

Phil had gotten out of his chair and made his way over to the ATV. He was leaning over in preparation of trying to throw his leg over the seat.

"Hey, little bro," Cog said. "Where are you going?"

"Phil," Clarke said. "What are you doing?"

"Thought . . ." He threw his leg up and got stuck there, his voice hissing.

Clarke went to him and started to pick him up to return him to his seat.

"Hey, maybe your brother wants a turn," Cog said. "You . . . krrssshh . . . krrsshhhh . . . turn . . ." he said, mocking Phil's manner of speech.

Clarke turned on his friend again, ready to do more than throw him off a cliff.

Cog put his hands up in a pose of surrender at the same time that Phil said, "Clarke . . ." distracting Clarke for a moment. Cog leapt around him and picked up Phil, holding him above his head in both hands.

Clarke leapt onto the ATV, using its height to jump over Cog's head, grabbing his brother in a tackle, and falling with the one-armed robot to the ground, rolling, coming back up and throwing himself at Cog, his bare right hand clamping on his friend's throat while the other hand tore through Cog's shirt into his simul-flesh.

Cog tore at Clarke's face, but his still flesh-covered hands couldn't tear the same way that Clarke's metal ones could. "Come on," Cog said. "Come on. You want to?"

"You stay the fuck away from my brother," Clarke said.

"Brother? He's a freak-show junk heap. The ATV has more going for it."

Phil put his one hand on Clarke's shoulder. "No, no, no, no . . ." Phil was stuck again, and all of Clarke's anger turned—Beachstone, Mary's pain, Kent, Barren Cove—and he grabbed Phil in a way he hadn't since that first day on the beach when he'd torn off his brother's arm, and he hurled him over the cliff.

Cog laughed. "Man, you fucked up my chest," he said.

Clarke stared at the spot where Phil had gone over.

"I knew you were robo," Cog said, "but that was fucking awesome."

Clarke turned to look at his friend. His eyes saw the hand-made wheelchair instead, and he went and threw that off the cliff as well, and he screamed and played his prerecorded laugh, "Ha, ha, ha, ha, ha." He held both hands out to either side of him and ran through the fingers, one at a time in sequence and back again.

He looked at Cog, who was watching him with great respect, and then he leapt off the edge, forming a perfect dive, landing in a roll, and coming up on his feet, a move he'd practiced many times.

Phil was lying facedown several feet away, the wheelchair nearby as well. The broken robot's legs were jerking, causing a horrible grinding sound. The shoulder gears were spinning, of course, the sand spraying where they touched the ground.

Clarke was horrified. Look at him. Exactly the same as that first day on the beach almost two months ago, jerking and seizing in the sand, no different, nothing changed, and to what end?

Cog landed somewhere behind him and approached, but he was with it enough to know not to say anything. Instead they stood there, listening to the ever present sound of the water and the grinding of gears, until eventually the gears stopped.

"What happened?" Cog said.

"His battery died," Clarke said.

"His battery!"

Clarke glared at the big robot, who turned his head away. Then Clarke bent down, picked Phil up, and started walking along the beach in the direction of Barren Cove. He left the wheelchair where it was, shouldering the weight himself, bringing his brother home.

19.

KAPEC AND CLARKE dug the grave. Mary watched from the upstairs window. The day was beautiful. What she could see of the ocean from the house was placid, a deep blue line just below the blue of the sky. When she stopped to listen, she could always hear the ocean churning from anywhere near Barren Cove, but from the house itself, she never saw the waves, only the water that was far enough from shore as to be some other in-between place of calm and quiet. Now, the sound of the grave being dug floated up to her, even through the window. As she watched, the hole grew deep enough that Clarke jumped in with his shovel. Kapec stopped—there wasn't enough room in the grave for both of them—and leaned against his own shovel, watching Clarke work. She could imagine that Kapec was fretting over the destruction of his beautiful lawn. He would be out with the seed later that afternoon, no doubt. For now, he stooped to shape the mound of dirt beside the hole, smoothing it, unable to leave even a pile of dirt lumpy and uneven.

Mary had been worried that they would dig up Asimov 3000 or worse, Master Vandley, and with each shovelful of dirt, she felt relieved. Their unmarked cemetery. Their backyard.

"Have they finished yet?"

She could hear Beachstone limping toward her, but she didn't turn away from the window. "No," she said.

He stopped short of being able to see out the window. If she had counted his steps correctly, he was five feet behind her. "Well, let me know when they're ready."

The sound of the shovel hitting the dirt reached them. Crunch. The sound of the dirt hitting the mound followed. Thump.

Mary watched. Clarke worked with the same even movements, like clockwork. She wondered why Beachstone's limp had become more pronounced. She couldn't help but feel that it was affected, and yet, what did she really know about human mechanics? Every human was an individual, and so all the medical texts in the world couldn't tell her anything about Beachstone. She still had the same fascination with him she'd had when she first saw the boy limping all those years ago. What was pain?

Beachstone sat on the bed behind her.

Crunch. Thump.

"Does your leg hurt terribly?" Mary said.

"No, no, I'm fine," Beachstone said.

"We haven't run out of aspirin yet."

"I'm fine."

Mary had noticed that Mr. Brown was getting older, that his store was less fully stocked, that nobody else was ever there when she went for supplies. She hadn't said anything to Beachstone yet, and Beachstone never went to town. There was still time before she had to make other arrangements.

"It's finally over," Beachstone said from the bed. He waited. "You know this is the right thing to do."

"I don't know that," Mary said.

"It is the right thing to do."

Clarke was lower in the hole now, probably up to his shoulders. Graves had been dug deep to prevent disease as the biodegradable corpses rotted. How deep did a robot's grave need to be? They had made Asimov 3000's the requisite six feet.

"Mary, come here," Beachstone said.

Mary didn't turn.

"I failed us. It is my failure. But I'm sorry."

Crunch. Thump. Kapec stopped the flow of the dirt from the mound back into the grave with his shovel. He scooped some up and tossed it onto the other side of the mound. Clarke changed the angle at which he was digging.

"And Clarke," Beachstone's tone hardened, "that sadistic little shit, to make a mockery of our son! Our son!" The last a rasp.

Mary spun. She must have looked shocked, because Beachstone's manner softened at once. "He's my son, too," Mary managed, just above a whisper.

Beachstone nodded. "I know. He's our—"

"*Clarke* is my son, too."

Beachstone's eyes narrowed. "No."

Mary willed herself to meet his gaze.

"What filial love he's shown then," Beachstone said. "Torturing you with this. Weeks of dragging that—" He stopped himself.

Whatever he had been about to say hung between them.

"Come sit with me, Mary." It sounded like a demand, but she knew he was upset and needed to be comforted, just like a child. Only Mary got to see that. His face looked blank. He probably thought that it looked pained. "I'm sorry, Mary," he said. He held out his hands to her, reaching.

She stepped within range, and he latched onto her, burying his head in her middle.

"We still could fix him," she said. "I could do the mechanics. Even Clarke—"

He jerked his head back. "No!"

"Did you ever think Clarke cared for Philip out of brotherly love?"

"Clarke! Don't fool yourself."

Mary closed her eyes and paused. This was about Philip. "We could still fix him."

Beachstone buried himself in her again. "No," he said softly into her stomach.

"He didn't ask for this. And there's no reason something couldn't be done."

"No," Beachstone said, pulling away. "No. Don't you understand? He was supposed to be ours." He patted the bed. "Sit down here."

Mary just looked down at him. She understood. She understood all too well. And that was why she didn't understand how he didn't see that by burying their son they were admitting something. And what was worse, she was worried he was willing to sacrifice whatever hope they had of salvaging their dream as an act of spite for Clarke's benefit.

"This was supposed to be ours," Beachstone said. He closed his eyes and shook his head, trying to see what he wanted to say. He stood up. "I know that it was my fault, but I was hoping that you would . . . that you could . . . just, well . . . I'm still here." He grabbed ahold of her, his arms tightened around her neck, and he brought his mouth to her ear. "I'm still right here.

We're still both here. We still have each other. I have you." He squeezed even harder.

Mary was surprised at his strength. He was so spindly. He was still sick so often. He redoubled his hold on her neck. A human would have choked, Mary thought. A human would have said, *Wait*, while prying at his arm, and he would have had to let go, just a little bit or he would have strangled her, but she allowed him to continue hugging her. She wanted to be held. He still hugged like he was a little child. Had she grown?

Beachstone pulled back. He looked toward the window. There had been the thump of the dirt hitting the mound, but there had been no crunch of the shovel sinking back into the dirt. Clarke was too low perhaps. They both paused in the silence. No new thump came. Beachstone took his cane and started toward the window. "They must be done."

"We could fix him," Mary said one last time. She kept her voice neutral, purposely robotic.

"No," he said, without looking at her. "They're finished." He started toward the door. When she didn't fall in step beside him, he stopped and looked back at her. "Come," he said, holding out his hand.

She stepped forward, allowing him to loop her arm in his. He leaned against her, and she knew that he was exaggerating his weakness. He had stood on his own only the moment before. He was still young. He was healthy for once. But she was a daughter leading her father. She was a bride being walked down the aisle. They had to part to go through the door and she fell behind him in the hallway.

Clarke was just mounting the stairs as they reached the top step. He stepped back, giving them the right of way. Beachstone passed Clarke without a word. He dug our son's grave, Mary wanted to say, regardless of whatever else you thought, but there was no reason to call attention to their pettiness. "I was just going up to get him," Clarke said as she passed.

"Is Kent coming?" Mary said.

"He couldn't decide. But he'll be there." He bounded up the stairs.

All this work, Mary thought. Beachstone would say it was morbid enjoyment in staging his own little funeral. Let's dig a grave! We'll bury someone too! It was true that most of the time it seemed the boy respected no one. That was no doubt inherited from his father, but she had meant what she'd said about brotherly love. Or she wanted to—a piece of her in him. It gave her some comfort as she went out to bury her second son.

Why hadn't she realized how poor a job Beachstone had done when she was doing the programming? Beachstone had said it was all his fault, and she hadn't corrected him. But she should have known. But then, maybe she had known and hadn't wanted to correct him then either.

Beachstone stepped out into the backyard and Mary stepped down behind him. He turned, offering his arm, and this time, when she took it, she felt as though he had intended to support her. She had brooded upstairs. He knew that. He felt guilty. Well, good. She wanted to mourn Philip. The old human saying was that a parent should never have to bury a child. Her father had understood that. He had had Beachstone, though. There should never have been any reason for Mary to understand losing someone this way. She wanted to scream for a moment: he didn't ask for this! She messaged Kent instead.

"Neither did you," Kent messaged back. He didn't turn from beside Kapec at the graveside. "Don't you feel almost human?"

She didn't answer him but led, or was led by, Beachstone to a spot just beside her brother.

A bit of dirt slid from the top of the mound and rained into the grave. Kapec smacked the mound with his shovel. "He's good parts still, even if you don't want him," he said.

Mary looked at Beachstone, afraid of his reaction, but he acted as though he hadn't heard.

"Don't think they bury anyone in the cities anymore. They don't even bury the humans. They just burn them."

Why wasn't anyone stopping him? The gardener!

Clarke came out of the house carrying Philip in his arms. He had rested the removed arm in Philip's lap. Mary wondered where he had kept it; she hadn't seen it since activation day, all those hours standing in Clarke's doorway, watching Philip charge, torturing herself. Philip's neck was rigid, his head still upright.

"Damn shame," Kapec said, but even he seemed to have the sense to be quiet.

Clarke walked right up to the edge of the grave and jumped in. He bent down and placed Philip on the ground with such tenderness that Mary knew she had been right. There *was* love there. Then he ruined it by looking up at Beachstone with a mean smile, a hateful gloat.

"There should have been a coffin," Kent said.

"What?" Beachstone said.

"You should have built a coffin. A box to put him in."

"We didn't for Father," Mary said.

Clarke climbed out of the grave. Philip was lying in the bottom of the hole. His arm still lay on his stomach. Wires protruded from the open socket of his shoulder. The grinding of his gears had been something terrible. It was so unnatural. And his voice, so mechanical.

Kapec started brushing the dirt back into the hole. It filled the side of the grave between Philip's body and the grave wall.

"Wait!" Beachstone said.

Kapec stopped and looked at Beachstone, his shovel arrested midair.

"We should say something."

"To another human fuckup," Clarke said, his eyes glued to the robot in the ground.

"Clarke, behave," Mary messaged.

"But haven't I, Mother?" he messaged back. "Better than anyone."

She flinched. She steadied Beachstone even though he hadn't moved.

"The young are wasted on us," Kent said. "We can't really understand youth, because, after all, aren't we forever young ourselves? Wasn't there a time when I wasn't at all? Philip is again at that time. I didn't know him. Those of us here who did knew him well enough to want to say good-bye with such formality. I can only hope . . . Rest in peace—that's what is said, right?"

"Yes," Mary said. She became aware that Beachstone was crying. He was silent but his breathing had changed. She turned her head just enough to see him, and she saw the tears streaming down his face. A dribble of snot drained from one nostril and beaded at the rise of his lip.

"He's crying," Kent group messaged.

"Have you seen this before?" Clarke group messaged. He stared openly.

"Yes," Mary responded, and then realized that doing so had been a kind of betrayal. The robots all stood in silence as Beachstone cried. He squeezed Mary's arm tighter, and she felt lucky in that moment. She let her momentary sense of guilt go and relished the fact that he needed her. He gestured with his arm, and when he did, his breath escaped from between his closed lips. He gasped, and there was the wet sound of saliva or maybe his dripping nose. Kapec, silent and respectful, understood the gesture and began pushing the dirt from the mound into the grave. It began to cover Philip's body now. Clarke picked up his shovel and began throwing full shovelfuls into the grave. Crunch, thump, only now, up close, the thump was accompanied by the spray of the dirt as it broke apart and settled. It blended with the sound of the ocean from below.

The dirt began to cover Philip's body. Mary understood now why people had built coffins before, and it wasn't for the same disease-preventing reasons that they had buried their dead. It was because it was unnatural for someone to be buried under the ground. She expected Philip to sit up at any moment and brush off the dirt and chastise them for trying to bury him. His arm was pushed from his body by one of the shovelfuls of dirt. It fell next to his body and rested half on him and half submerged.

Beachstone gasped for breath. Mary envied him his physical emotions. She could feel her brother's awe. Beachstone looked at all of them, turned, and walked away.

Mary waited a moment. Philip's face was still uncovered, but parts of him were completely hidden by the dirt. She turned and followed after Beachstone. He was nearly at the house. See, he must not need to limp as badly as he lets on, she thought. She caught up with him just inside the kitchen. He turned to her. His face was red, his eyes wet, tears and snot ready to fall from his chin. He grabbed her head in both of his hands. "I love you," he said. "You know that. I will always love you."

She nodded, wishing she could message him.

"We tried," he said, and with that he turned. As he crossed the kitchen, he wiped his face with his shirtsleeve.

She was always trying, Mary wanted to say. Always.

From outside, the sounds of the day were loud again. Crunch, thump. Only now, as Clarke and Kapec worked together, the sound overlapped, crun-crun-thu-crun-thu-crunch. Thump. Thump.

20.

IT BECAME INCREASINGLY essential to me that I meet my landlord, Beachstone. The information I had heard from Dean, the collective conscience of Barren Cove, had one noticeable gap—Beachstone's human mind had never been recorded. The man who was described seemed complex—sickly, yet strong of will; brooding, yet full of love—and his longevity, while so much at Barren Cove had clearly changed, only further served as a point of interest. Humans had a knack for dying. Yet Beachstone lived on. The Kent I had met bore no resemblance to the Kent who had forced Beachstone to live in the very building that I myself now lived in. The Mary Dean described had a greater complexity than the brittle, beautiful shell who had tried to play hostess. I was eager to measure those changes myself, yet to understand Barren Cove, and even my own place there, I felt that I had to tap the one resource that might not always be available to me. I determined to find entry to Beachstone's chamber. I regretted that I had been stopped by Kent the night that Clarke had nearly tossed my arm from the cliff. I figured it was reasonable to believe that I could now claim various invitations to the house, especially given the length of time I had avoided contact since my nightmarish foray into town with Clarke. I called on Barren Cove to find out.

The house was still, even from the outside. I looked up at it from the top of the cliff stairs, wondering why it seemed so quiet. I realized that Kapec was not to be seen. There was no sound of water running, or a mower buzzing, no sound other than the distant call of the ocean below. A curtain moved in one of the back upper rooms. I couldn't be sure who the figure was, but there was somebody at home. All at once, I was struck with the feeling of my own isolation. Where was I? No place with nobody. Everything here was static. Even the things that moved were static—the ocean, Kapec, even the higher-order robots like Clarke—a constant coming and going, banging against the shore, walking over the grounds, going to town. What were my own rhythms here? I didn't feel as though I had any, and yet, hadn't I climbed these stairs and gone to this house before? Could I so easily trade one life for another?

I realized that I had been waiting for the curtain to move again. When it didn't, I started around to the front of the house. There was nothing there either. I opened the front door without knocking. There was no need for propriety here. Nobody was downstairs.

"Should I alert Mary to your arrival?" Dean asked.

I thought back on the last time I had been in the house, when Kent had stopped me just outside Beachstone's door. There was no reason I couldn't show myself up to my landlord's room. Could it have been his room in which the curtain had moved? No, it was the wrong side of the house.

"No. I've come to see Beachstone," I said. "I know the way." With that, I started for the stairs, in part to back up my statement, but just as much to convince myself that barging into other people's homes wasn't wrong. If I was supposed to reflect on my being and reasons for living, then breaking old mores would help me understand myself better.

"You shouldn't do that without Mary's permission."

I ignored Dean and walked straight to the end of the hall, opening Beachstone's door with no hesitation. A gaunt human form lay beneath the covers on a large four-poster bed. Mary sat on the edge of the bed beside him. The human was lying flat on his back, his eyes closed, his long hair white, his face shrunken and wrinkled. At first I was quite sure that he was dead. Then the sheet rose ever so slightly as his lungs took in air. And Mary turned to face me in shock. Her hand stopped halfway to her opened mouth, a gesture so human as to once again give me the eerie sensation that she couldn't possibly be a robot herself.

"There was no one downstairs," I said, knowing that this was a weak argument; why hadn't I had Dean call? I stepped forward. As I spoke, my eyes fixed on the unconscious Beachstone, both fascinated and repulsed by his illness. "I wanted to meet my landlord. I thought we might have quite a lot to say to each other." My landlord was clearly not in a state to say anything to anybody. And yet, still I walked forward.

Mary stood up and held her hand out. "Don't," she said.

"What's wrong with him?" I said.

"Please go. Now. You can't be in here."

"Is he okay?" I said. Of course he wasn't okay. Perhaps I meant, would he be okay? I had never seen such an old human. I had thought the man that Clarke and his friends had beaten had been old, but this was a truly old man. I looked behind me to see if Clarke was there. His gruesome face would have seemed sacrilegious in Beachstone's presence. The hall behind me was empty.

Mary had started around the bed. "Get out of here now," she said.

I looked at her and she stopped. We both came to ourselves.

I was in the wrong place. It was not my place to be there. I started toward the door. "I'm sorry," I said.

Mary stood watching me go, forlorn.

I looked back at the figure on the bed. It frightened me. I stepped into the hall, and Mary rushed forward, slamming the door. I had shamed us all. I couldn't stay here. I had come to be alone, to be myself, to answer some questions, but instead I had plunged into the world of Barren Cove. I wasn't asking questions about me, I was asking questions about them, and in so doing, I had broken into their house and broken into their already broken lives.

The hall was dark. I started for the stairs. "Don't be upset," a voice said as I passed one of the open rooms. I turned to find Kent—fat, effeminate Kent. "She's terribly possessive." He was winding the key on a reproduction toy robot. He stooped and set the toy down. When he let go, it began to jerk forward, slowly, painfully slowly, its gears buzzing, its feet playing leapfrog with themselves.

"I just wanted to see," I said.

"And now you have seen," Kent said, looking up from his toy to me, executing a perfect smile. "Isn't it adorable?"

I thought at first that he had meant Beachstone, and I was repulsed by the word, but then I saw that he had meant the toy. "It's insulting."

"Like Rosie," he said, knowingly.

It was the same answer I had given on my first day here. I hadn't changed at all.

"Insulting because it's a reminder," he said, holding out his hands to either side as though he had just executed a magic trick. "As is Beachstone. What will Mary do without him?"

"Is he alive?"

"Yes. For now. But all living things . . ." He glanced toward the window and then went to it, looking out. Had it been Kent behind the curtain? It occurred to me that the story he had told me in the cabana, so full of genuine emotion and passion, was nothing more than a preprogrammed memory written by Beachstone. Kent had not remembered his time in the city, but rather, a time that had been remembered for him. That was Beachstone's voice behind Kent's story. Was it so different from the story that Dean had told me? Kent was still handed all the blame. But Mary and Beachstone's love was legitimized. There was Michael and there was Jennifer, and when they were gone there was nobody left but Mary and Beachstone. But Beachstone wasn't satisfied with that. He had taken Kent's son away from him. Clarke was somebody else's. The degree to which Beachstone had taken his revenge was frightening; perhaps he was no more enlightened than we were.

Still, I didn't like how smug Kent seemed now. Wasn't he younger than I was, and here he was with his little toys, so certain about life. "What about Clarke?" I said.

"Ah, Dean has been talking, haven't you old girl?" Kent said. Dean was silent. "Yes, everything is a reminder of something. Of course, we can't remember everything." The toy robot on the floor had wound down, stopping midstep, one leg raised. "Have you been enjoying your time here?"

I thought of the dying figure down the hall, and I wanted

to be gone from there. I needed to be back outside. Everything might have been a reminder of something, but just then Barren Cove seemed little better than a house of dead memories, a tomb.

"Come sit with me," Kent said.

I was supposed to meet Jenny at noon, but that was still hours away. I thought of going back to the cabana and remembered Kent calling it dismal. I had begun to feel that he was right. It was too cramped. It didn't merely provide a place to think, but became a place in which there was nothing to do but to think.

Dean's story of Barren Cove was fascinating to me, and I couldn't help but feel that there were answers in it. And yet, the things that I knew that had taken place within these walls—the sickness of the place—even the sickness I had seen with my own eyes, made me feel as though I wasn't actually learning anything of value for myself. I was, rather, wallowing in somebody else's pain to disguise my own. The ocean teemed with life. But Barren Cove served to emphasize the futility of it all. In the city, there was a fevered pitch to life that didn't allow time for reflection. I had already learned that the ocean didn't say, *Hush, hush*, but rather, *Why? Why?*

Kent sat on a bench at the end of the bed now.

"I need to go."

"Don't worry about Mary. She won't be coming out of there for a long time. Come." He patted the seat next to him.

What had we been saying to each other? The toy robot was inert on the floor. Kent's dog was hidden in a corner, shut down. "I've got to go," I said, and I backed out of the room. I was afraid that Kent was going to pursue me, but I walked downstairs and out into the sunshine without being stopped. The gardens were still without their gardener. Where was Clarke? Did he even stay at the house anymore?

I hurried around to the cliff steps. What had I seen? Was this why Asimov 3000 had deactivated? To avoid the sight of Beachstone's deathbed? I was suddenly all of them, first Kent, now Asimov 3000; was I somehow Mary too? Did their drama need an audience?

The old man was dying. His life was imperceptible. I thought about Jenny's invitation and decided to find the clearing even if I would be early. It was better than being alone with my failings.

The weather at Barren Cove had an uncanny temper, changing moods at the slightest provocation. As I set out, the sky was pristine, the breeze off the ocean just right. I took the weather to be a fortuitous sign. Now it seems that it would have been more appropriate if it had stormed that day. It was almost as if Barren Cove had finally turned its back on its inhabitants.

I headed straight for town while scanning the edge of the woods for any sign of a path. I began to despair that the way would be hidden, that I would never find my way to the clearing, and that I would miss my one opportunity at—what? Happiness?—no, but at least a chance to have a few moments of comfort. It was when I was contemplating turning back, fully aware that I had been tricked, the victim of another practical joke by bored young robots, that Jenny appeared up ahead. She zoomed toward me, soaring past me, then circled around, laughing. "I thought you might not be coming," she said.

"I didn't know where I was going."

"Doesn't everybody know where the clearing is?"

"Everybody but me."

She continued to circle and I turned in place, following her. The world spun, a blur in the background.

"Stop for a moment," I said.

"But it's so much fun watching you turn."

I stopped then, resisting the urge to look over my shoulder at her. "Come here."

She pulled in front of me, leaning toward me, offering her cheek. I reached out a hand, wanting to feel her face—it looked so smooth, so pale. She pulled away at the last minute, laughing. "You're a dirty old man."

I felt snubbed. "Then why'd you invite me here?"

"Because you're cute," she said. She grabbed my hand and pulled. "Come on," she said. She scooted in close to me, one of her tires going between my legs, her body only inches from mine. "Not here," she whispered. And then she was pulling on my hand again. I allowed myself to be pulled forward, once again enjoying being teased. Jenny kept looking back at me as she led the way, and I could tell she was impatient with my speed, but I figured it was only fair that she had to wait too. My mind felt clear in a way that was so foreign I was almost distracted by it. I wasn't thinking about life, the city, Barren Cove; I wasn't even registering the trees soaring by or the position of the sun in the sky; I was blinded by the flashes of white skin alternating with pink hair and the sound of her laughter. I had the thought *This was what I was missing*, and then I was consumed in the moment again.

"Would you hurry?" Jenny said.

"You're pulling me as fast as I can go."

She stopped. "Well, hop on and I'll drive you."

"No." I shook my head. "You can wait too."

Her eyes flashed. She growled and snapped her teeth at me, and then started pulling me along again.

We came to a break in the trees that was so subtle that I probably would have missed it. The undergrowth at the edge of the forest blocked the entrance to the path, but once we stepped past that undergrowth, there was a narrow clear path of beaten dirt that ran straight back through the trees. Jenny's tires crackled over the twigs and dry leaves on the forest floor. She stopped in the middle of the path and turned back to me.

"Is this it?" I said. We were just far enough down the path that the edge of the forest was hidden from normal vision.

"No, silly," she said, laughing at me again. I entertained her, and yet that didn't insult me. Was I quaint? Was I old? I wondered if she had ever been to the city; if she had any idea what I had seen; if she would be so amused if she realized how provincial she really was. She held up two memory chips.

"Sims?" I said.

"Of course," she said, extending one toward me.

"Wait," I said, grabbing her wrist. "I want us to be with it for this."

"No, man, it's a party." She wrenched her wrist from my grip and slid the memory chip into her own port. Her pupils dilated; she swayed a moment and giggled.

I took the other chip and inserted it in my port. It wasn't like the first time. Everything just grew brighter, and I felt as though it was even harder to focus on anything but Jenny. When she moved her hand, there was an afterimage that trailed from her fingers. She turned and started down the path. I followed. Everything blurred around me.

The clearing appeared with little warning. It was sunny. Jenny turned as soon as we were off the path and placed her hands on my shoulders. "Your face is like beauty," she said.

"You are beautiful," I said.

I was running my hands up and down her sides, darting up

to touch her face and her hair. I felt her hand at my port and stopped for a second. "Whoa, wait."

"What?" she said.

"I'm not—I mean . . ." I wasn't sure what I was trying to say.

"Silly, it's just for fun," she said, and slipped her USB plug into my port, connecting us.

So this is it, I thought . . . but then I felt as though I had been flooded with numbers. It wasn't her USB plug at all. We weren't connected. She was getting me drunk. The afterimage that seemed to accompany every object grew in intensity so that it was hard to differentiate between trees, the ground, the leaves, Jenny, me. "I love you," I said.

Jenny burst out laughing. She sounded hysterical, and yet there was also something sinister beneath it. "Ha, ha, ha, ha, ha."

"I love you," I said again, unable to stop myself.

Jenny stepped back, bringing her hands to her mouth as she continued to laugh.

"Ha, ha, ha, ha, ha."

But her hands also seemed to still be at her sides.

"You are too much," she said.

She grew in size. No, there was somebody else beside her.

"Ha, ha, ha, ha, ha."

I realized then why the laugh sounded sinister. It was because Jenny's laugh had been mixing with Clarke's. But the clearing had been empty when we came into it. Hadn't it? Clarke turned Jenny to face him, and then he bent her over almost completely backward and kissed her fully on the mouth, a human kiss, a show. There was a glow around them, but I could see clearly enough. His hands were firm on her back. She brought her hands up to his head and kissed him back.

"No," I said.

When I thought that they had made their point, they still didn't stop. Jenny gripped him with intensity.

It had been a practical joke after all. I was just a target for their boredom. They had used up their humans and so now at least they had a human-made robot to mock. Humiliate. "Enough," I said.

They didn't stop.

"That's enough."

Clarke brought his hand to her port, revealing his USB plug. Would they? Right in front of me?

"Help."

I looked up at the sky. The sun blew out my photoreceptors; it was a starburst. White.

"Help!"

Clarke and Jenny had not broken their kiss when my visual came back online. "Stop," I said. They didn't know who they were messing with. They didn't know what I was capable of. But was I really capable of anything more than self-destruction? "Help!" Why weren't they listening to me? But it wasn't me, was it? Had I been calling for help? Clarke and Jenny broke their kiss and turned to face me, their arms around each other's waists.

"Sorry, old man," Clarke said. "It was just too good to resist."

"You're evil," I said.

"Tell me you didn't get some pleasure out of it."

I had. In the beginning. Was this humiliation worth it?

Jenny approached me, and she brought her lips to mine. It wasn't the same passionate kiss that she and Clarke had shared, just a peck, an acknowledgment. But it forced me to admit that the feeling I'd had before Clarke appeared had been worth the humiliation.

"At least you got fucked up," Jenny said.

"Why?"

"Mary, would you freaking get over it!" Clarke yelled.

I was confused. Mary? "Help," I heard again, and realized that it was Mary's voice. That it had not been my own cry. She had sent out a group message. "If you are near town, please go to Marvin Brown. Beachstone's sick; he needs his medicine."

"We better go," I said.

"Beachstone's always sick," Clarke said. Jenny was by his side again. He stood to the side of her, one hand on her tummy, the other on her back. He nuzzled her neck. They still glowed, which made it worse.

"But shouldn't we—"

"Do what you want, old man."

I stepped toward him. I wanted to deactivate him right there. I was just a proxy for him. He couldn't bring himself to attack Beachstone, because it would hurt his mother, so he killed humans and toyed with human-built robots. Jenny blew me a kiss. I turned away and started down the path.

But it was a hard path to follow. The undergrowth twined together. Everything was moving. "I'm nearly in town," I messaged to Dean to forward to Mary. I burst out of the edge of the forest and the open space was more disorienting than the trees. How long did the sim last? How long had it lasted last time? I stumbled toward town, which I could see as an outline on the horizon. I was filled with anger still. I wanted to run from it, but it kept renewing itself inside me. It wasn't just the jealousy, although that was a large part of it. It was the way in which they had crushed my hope. It was how good Jenny had made me feel, off and on, from the first day I arrived at Barren Cove, right up until Clarke stepped out of the shadows; it was the way that I thought maybe there was a reason to go on living after all. And the way they proved how evil the world has really become.

What was the point? Beachstone must surely have known. He had to know. Facing every day knowing that it could be his last. It had to make every moment precious. Why else would he still be alive? I had to see him again and make him talk. He was useless silent. But if he stayed alive . . .

"I'm coming," I sent out again.

"Help! Help! Help!"

"I'm coming." I had to save him. I had to save him. That was all I knew. I had to save him. So he could tell me. Because— Clarke kicking John Gropner flashed in my head—the death of humanity was the devolution of the robots.

I came into town. The buildings all vibrated, but they didn't move. The sim must have been wearing off. It was the first time I had been in town during the day. There was light activity in the streets. A robot cut the grass in front of a house. Two other robots were repainting a house that seemed to shine with new paint already. I passed a robot on its hands and knees in the middle of the street. It appeared to be picking up pebbles and putting them into a canvas sack.

I needed Marvin Brown. I didn't know where to look.

Many robots sat on their front porches or the stairs that led up to their houses. They didn't talk to each other, at least not out loud; they didn't seem to be doing anything. They just sat.

"Help!" the message came again.

"I've answered her," I yelled. But still the continued urgency made me nervous. I was going to fail. I was never going to find out why. Why wouldn't the buildings stop vibrating? I needed Marvin Brown.

Another robot was kneeling in the street ahead of me. I was confused. Was this what they did all day? I would ask him where Marvin Brown was. But then, as I got nearer, I saw that it wasn't a robot at all. It was John Gropner's body. It had been left where we had beaten him. The blood was rust colored where it had dried on his skin. An animal of some kind must have been eating the body, because his cheek had been gouged out. I felt as though I had already failed in my task. I looked around, panicked now. Two male robots sat on different steps leading up to one of the nearby houses. I approached the edge of the lawn. "I'm looking for Marvin Brown," I said.

There was a pause. I wondered if I had spoken at all. I thought maybe I needed to message. They still talked out loud out here, didn't they? Then one of the robots pointed back in the direction I had come. "Down by town center. You'll see his place. Still has a sign out front that says Brown's."

I hurried back down the street, passing the robot picking up pebbles and coming to the town center. The fountain was running, and two robots stood beside it, watching the water cascade in symmetric arcs.

Brown's appeared to be an old storefront. I hurried to the door and tried it but found it locked. I knocked. "Hello? Hello?" I yelled, which at some point turned to, "Help, help!"

The door finally slid open and a robot stood in the door-way.

"Marvin Brown, please," I said.

"I'm Marvin Brown."

I had expected a human, even though I knew that they were supposed to all be dead. "I need medicine for Beachstone. He's sick. Mary sent me."

"He's always sick," Marvin Brown said. But he turned back into the store. I followed him inside. There were empty shelves and faded advertisements. Brown went behind what had once been a counter and came up with a small bottle that rattled as he moved it. "Here," he said, handing it to me.

I took it and said, "Thank you."

"Mary's got to learn to relax. Sending her tenant just isn't right."

"Thank you," I said again. Marvin Brown glowed. He seemed like an angel to me. I wanted to hug him. I wanted to kiss him.

"It's just not right."

"I was in town anyway," I said.

Brown didn't say anything to that, and I turned and left.

Outside, nothing had changed. The robots still lounged around or watched the water. It seemed like a ghost town. I suddenly missed the city. I missed the traffic. I missed the stores, the crowds, the illusion of life. I began to run. Motion lines still shot out of every object, and as I ran it seemed as though the world was moving and not I. I remembered riding Jenny the first night we went into town. I felt as though I could move that fast now. I ran. The pills in the bottle rattled as I ran. I would make it. I would save him.

One human life. There had been a time when robots would have died to save one human life. He would tell me what I needed to know.

Barren Cove rose on the horizon. It was larger than I remembered, larger than anything. It blotted out the sun; it was everything, visible from so far away, making its presence known and forcing anyone nearby to reckon with it. I set straight for the front door. Dean's voice reached me. "Do you have it?"

I messaged that I did. There was no response, no congratulations, nothing. I wondered. I was within normal visual range of the house, already on the part of the land that came under Kapec's domain, when Mary came running out of the house. I thought she was coming to meet me, to carry the medicine the last few yards. Part of me wanted to yell out, I have it, don't get in my way, and the other part of me knew that it was really not my place to make the delivery, and that I had no idea how to administer the medicine once it was brought to Beachstone. I held up the hand that held the medicine. "I've got it," I called.

Mary stopped and looked at me. I could see that she hadn't realized I was there. She turned and started around the house.

I was at the front porch now, but I followed her to the back. The sound of the ocean wafted up on the breeze. "Mary! I have-it, come on!" I yelled, messaging the same thing at the same time. But I stopped, fully aware of what Mary was doing, yet unable to believe my eyes.

Mary didn't stop when she came to the edge of the cliff, but plunged over the side, actually launching herself into space and disappearing before I had a chance to register the sight. There was no sense of mischief attached to that leap, like there had been when her son had done the same thing before my eyes months before. There was only finality.

"You're too late," Dean messaged me. The comment seemed so superfluous that I wanted to dismantle her right then.

Kapec turned at my side and started back for the house.

"Where are you going?" I asked.

"To get the shovel," he said without turning. "You might want to go down and get her. She'd want to be buried with him."

This statement, so matter-of-fact, so robotic, made it all very clear to me. I opened my hand and looked down at the bottle of medicine resting in my palm. It was useless to me now.

It would soon be useless to anybody. I had missed my chance at answers. And yet, I couldn't help but feel that Mary's plunge over the cliff was, in its way, all the answer I needed.

• • •

When Clarke appeared, the sim had run its course. He appeared small to me. Kent had a black kimono for the occasion. Clarke joined Kapec in digging in the backyard without a word. They were old hands at that.

I went down to the beach. Mary's body was relatively intact. Her skin had been torn badly. Each of the gashes, both clean and ragged, emphasized that the material was nothing better than an illusion. Her eyes had both shattered, leaving her sockets empty. She most likely could have been fixed with minimal work. Surely new eyes and skin could be ordered from Lifetime Mechanics Co., Ltd. But I knew that she was broken beyond that. I sat in my chair in the cabana watching the ocean lap against the shore.

When the grave had been dug, Dean informed me that it was time to begin. I picked up Mary's body and carried it up the stairs. Kent and Kapec each stood near the grave. Kapec fidgeted with the mound of dirt beside the gaping hole. Clarke was just emerging from the house with Beachstone in his arms. It was the first time that I had gotten a really good look at the man. He was small and withered, his skin loose on his bones, marked, multicolored—nothing like a robot at all. Clarke jumped into the grave and set down his body and then I handed Mary down to him as well.

I heard the sound of somebody crying. I turned to see Kent with a handkerchief to his eyes, although they were quite dry. The sound was real, though. As Clarke had done with his laugh, Kent had downloaded a recording of a real human's tears.

We were burying his sister and—would he say . . . his brother?

I thought again of the story he had told me weeks before. He had been left with nothing. Or perhaps, by being left with grief, he had more than any of us.

Clarke started filling the grave at once, and Kapec followed his lead. I expected Kent to protest, and I almost protested on his behalf. There should be something said. There should be some ceremony. But Kent just cried. Clarke and Kapec worked. I stood to the side, watching. It was as if I had been granted an opportunity to see firsthand part of the story that I had learned from Dean. This could just as well have been Philip's funeral. Only now, it somehow lacked and yet was overwhelmed by the same sense of tragedy.

The ground was flat in only twenty-four minutes. Clarke and Kapec walked away, taking their shovels with them.

"And so it goes," Kent said, dabbing at his dry eyes one more time. Then he too turned and went back to the house.

I stood over the bare patch of dirt. The sun was on its way down, casting the backyard in the shadow of the house. The ocean was dark now, but still vocal. I started toward the cliff stairs, on my way to the cabana.

I had hoped that Beachstone would be able to give me an answer about life and death. To have the human knowledge of your own end must be the most comforting feeling in the world. Instead, I was left with Mary's conviction, Kent's mimicry, and Clarke's robotic stoicism. It made my own decision no clearer.

How could I ask to be shut down? What would tomorrow be without me? I might be old, but my interest in humans didn't seem to extend to a desire to share their fate. Shouldn't I have known that before I even left the city? I had ordered my spare parts after all. It was the first thing I had thought to do after I had let the bus hit me.

No, I thought, sitting in the cabana, watching the black waves, I had not found the answers I was looking for at Barren Cove.